A strong rap came at their door.

"Girls, we need you now!" their father commanded. His tone was uncharacteristically loud and demanding. It galvanized the girls, including Anastasia, into a flurry of activity. In minutes they were out the door, walking rapidly between two bayonet-toting guards, along with the rest of their family, down the dimly lit hallway.

"I'm scared," Mashka whispered to Anastasia.

"Don't be," Anastasia replied, reaching behind her to squeeze Mashka's hand. "Everything will be fine."

"Once upon a Time" is Timeless with These Retold Tales:

Beauty Sleep
By Cameron Dokey

Midnight Pearls
By Debbie Viguié

Snow
By Tracy Lynn

Water Song
By Suzanne Weyn

The Storyteller's Daughter
By Cameron Dokey

Before Midnight
By Cameron Dokey

Golden
By Cameron Dokey

The Rose Bride
By Nancy Holder

Sunlight and Shadow
By Cameron Dokey

The Crimson Thread
By Suzanne Weyn

Belle
By Cameron Dokey

The Night Dance
By Suzanne Weyn

Wild Orchid
By Cameron Dokey

ONCE UPON A TIME

THE
Diamond Secret

BY SUZANNE WEYN

SIMON PULSE
New York   London   Toronto   Sydney

SIMON PULSE

An imprint of Simon & Schuster Children's Publishing Division

1230 Avenue of the Americas, New York, NY 10020

Copyright © 2009 by Suzanne Weyn

All rights reserved, including the right of
reproduction in whole or in part in any form.

SIMON PULSE and colophon are registered trademarks
of Simon & Schuster, Inc.

The text of this book was set in Adobe Jenson.

Manufactured in the United States of America

First Simon Pulse paperback edition June 2009

6 8 10 9 7

Library of Congress Control Number 2008932846

ISBN: 978-1-4169-7530-4

For Rae Weyn Gonzalez, who always loved Anastasia best

PROLOGUE

Yekaterinburg, Russia
Shortly after midnight, July 17, 1918

"Get up, Anastasia! We have to get dressed. Hurry! Wake up!" Anastasia Romanov blinked hard, struggling to come awake. Why was her older sister Tatiana bending beside her bed, shaking her shoulder?

Turning her head, she saw that her other two older sisters, Olga and Mashka, were rapidly changing from their white ruffled nightgowns into day clothes. Olga was quickly tucking her puff-sleeved blouse into her long, narrow blue skirt. Mashka tugged a long gray jumper over a blue blouse with belled sleeves. Olga had a ruffled blouse slung over her shoulder.

This was very strange. Where could they be going?

Anastasia checked the clock at her bedside. It

was one in the morning! "What's happening?" she murmured as she sat up.

"The White Russian Army is coming to save us, just as Father said they would," Olga told her, giddy with excitement.

"We're going to be out of this awful place soon!" Mashka exulted. "Thank goodness!"

"It's better here than it was in Siberia," Anastasia pointed out as she swung her bare feet onto the cold wooden floor.

"But not nearly as good as it was at the palace," Olga countered. "I can't wait to go home."

There came a knock on the door, and Tatiana opened it to their mother, an elegant woman whom all four of them resembled. She had delicate, fine-boned features and thick blond hair, which she wore piled on top of her head. Czarina Alexandra already had changed out of her nightclothes. "Girls, your father says to put on the special petticoats your grandmother had sewn for each of you."

"I thought those were just supposed to be for an emergency," Olga questioned. "Aren't we being saved?"

"The Red Army is moving us, and we don't want to leave the petticoats," Czarina Alexandra explained calmly.

"Why are they moving us?" Anastasia asked.

"Don't be thick," Olga scolded her. "They're making it difficult for the White Army to find us."

"I'll show you who's thick," Anastasia cried. She leaped at her sister and tickled her ribs until both of them fell on the bed laughing.

The czarina clapped her hands sharply. "Enough of your constant clowning, Anastasia!"

Anastasia instantly wiped the smile from her face. Her mother was normally slow to anger, so she was clearly being very serious. "Sorry, Mother."

"Olga is correct. We are indeed being moved to keep the White Army from finding and rescuing us. At least, I presume so," Czarina Alexandra informed them, "and though we are confident that those in the White Army who are loyal to us will be victorious, until then we must be careful."

"Careful of what?" Anastasia asked.

A cloud of worry passed over her mother's face. "Nothing in particular, but we are in the middle of a civil war, and in war anything can happen. So now hurry and put on those petticoats under your clothing. I will be back to get you shortly."

As soon as her mother had left, Anastasia tossed off her nightgown while her sisters got out of the clothing they'd already begun to put on. Tatiana found their petticoats at the bottom of a trunk they'd brought from the grand Peterhof Palace . . . into exile in Siberia, and now to their latest location, this drafty estate the Bolshevik Red Army had named "The House of Special Purpose."

The estate's "special purpose," Anastasia assumed, was to hold her father, Czar Nicholas, their mother, Alexandra, her siblings—her three sisters and younger brother, Alexei—and herself prisoner. Along with Alexei's physician and several servants, the Imperial family had been here for months, captives of this peasant uprising. Their father had assured them that this revolution and their captivity would be over before the end of the year and now, it seemed, he had been right.

Anastasia pulled on the full petticoat, made of white eyelet material from shoulder to waist and ruffled at the knee-length bottom. She noticed that she didn't fill hers out nearly as well as her more curvaceous older sisters. "This is ridiculous! I'm already seventeen! When am I going to catch up to the rest of you?" she fretted, holding out the bodice of her petticoat and gazing down despairingly at it.

"Probably never," Mashka taunted, pulling her jumper back over her head.

Anastasia swiped a roll of socks and a small rag doll off the dresser and stuck them in the bosom of the undergarment. "There!" she cried with a playful nod at her newly enhanced figure. "I've surpassed you already!"

"Stop playing, Anastasia!" Tatiana scolded. "Get dressed."

A strong rap came at their door. "Girls, we need you now!" their father commanded. His tone was uncharacteristically loud and demanding. It galvanized the girls, including Anastasia, into a flurry of activity. In minutes they were out the door, walking rapidly between two bayonet-toting guards, along with the rest of their family, down the dimly lit hallway.

"I'm scared," Mashka whispered to Anastasia.

"Don't be," Anastasia replied, reaching behind her to squeeze Mashka's hand. "Everything will be fine."

CHAPTER ONE
Grim Memories in a Gray City

Yekaterinburg, Russia
April 1919

Ivan Ivanovitch Navgorny's dark eyes snapped open.

Not that dream again! With darting glances he surveyed his shabby hotel room in the iron-mining town of Yekaterinburg. Convinced he truly was awake, he sighed with relief. The room was a pit, but it was better than his nightmare.

Walking to the grimy window, Ivan pulled back the stained curtain and gazed out at the gray sky looming above the square industrial buildings. How eerie to return to this grim proletariat city on the border of Siberia, after swearing he'd never be back. He and Sergei had been here for less than a week, and it was already too long.

Where *was* Sergei? His blanket had been tossed

1

off the slumping couch where he'd slept. Ivan guessed that his friend probably had gone to finally pay their overdue hotel bill.

Ivan rubbed the sleep from his eyes. Now that he was awake, Ivan recalled the dream only in fleeting images and murmured conversations, blessedly difficult to reconstruct. But even upon waking he could remember the gunfire in his dream, as it had been in real life.

Ivan knew what terrible memory he was reliving in his sleep.

He didn't like to think of the event if it could be avoided. He shut it out so vigilantly, so utterly, in his conscious waking state that the memory's only outlet was to creep in at night when he could not guard against it.

Guard against it.

Guarding.

He'd been a guard in the Red Army stationed here in Yekaterinburg at The House of Special Purpose, a villa acting as a jailhouse for the exiled Russian royal family, the Romanovs. Guarding was what he'd *thought* he was doing—guarding the imprisoned Czar Nicholas; his wife, Czarina Alexandra; and their five children: the grand duchesses Olga, Tatiana, Anastasia, and Marie—whom they all called Mashka—and their younger brother, Alexei.

Ivan had been a Red soldier with the Bolsheviks then, a true believer in the words of Vladimir Lenin and Leon Trotsky regarding the rights of the Russian workers. Those leaders had believed in the cause of communism and so did Ivan—at least he had believed in it back then.

The one thing Ivan was thankful for was that he had been stationed *outside* the basement early that fateful July seventeenth in 1918. The White Russian Army loyal to the czar was advancing on Yekaterinburg, and he'd thought the royal family, their physician, and three of their servants were just being hidden downstairs to keep the White Army from liberating them.

He'd had no idea what was about to happen.

But he'd cringed outside the door in helpless disbelief when he'd heard the gunfire abruptly erupt, and he had imagined the horrible killings going on inside. Later, his imaginings had been augmented by unwelcome details told to him by soldiers who had fired the shots there in the basement. Ivan had tried to stopper his ears, to shut out their stories, but they had insisted, as though in an attempt to unload the burden of their own horror and guilt over what they'd done.

He understood how the rumor that Anastasia was still alive had started. She must have survived the first round of shootings—all three sisters had. They'd worn petticoats with so many jewels sewn into the waistbands that the gems had served as a kind of body armor, causing the bullets to bounce all over the room. Ivan's soldier comrades had told him that they themselves had had to jump away, shielding their heads, to avoid being struck.

There were no bouncing bullets the second time the soldiers fired.

When the dust had cleared, Czar Nicholas, Czarina Alexandra, Alexei, Olga, Tatiana, Mashka, and Anastasia were all found lying silently in a heap.

Then the soldiers had collected the scattered jewels and had ripped at the seams of the dead family's clothes, searching for more hidden treasure, which they found. Then they had enlisted Ivan's help to take the bodies to the woods to bury.

In the woods, Ivan had stood guard beside the body of Anastasia while the other soldiers had dug graves. Her hair was over her face. Her summer dress had been torn away and now revealed the waist of her bullet-scorched petticoat.

Before that moment, Ivan had seen Anastasia only at a distance as she walked in the garden of The House of Special Purpose. Back then, he hadn't been able to get a close look at her, but he could tell she was a lively soul from the way her slim form danced along the walkways with her sisters, sometimes teasing, often laughing.

To see her so still . . . it was a horror that had sickened him to the very depths of his being.

Stepping away, Ivan had vomited heavily into a bush.

When he turned back, his heart had skipped.

Anastasia—the corpse he'd viewed just a moment before—was pulling herself forward, clawing her way across the dirt.

He'd watched in speechless disbelief, wondering if he possibly could be imagining it.

Tensing as she sensed him watching her, Anastasia had stopped and swung her head around to him.

Through the tangle of hair that veiled most of her face, her eyes had spoken to him, begging him not to reveal her.

He gave his tacit agreement by turning his back to her and bending forward, pretending to heave his guts out once more.

Ivan never questioned his complicity in her escape, not even for a second. If she could manage, by some implausible combination of ferocious will and improbable luck, to escape this atrocious and premature death, he would not be the one to alert the others. The true believer in the Communist cause he had once been had died, just as surely as the Romanovs had been slaughtered.

Glancing back, he had seen that she was getting farther away.

The summer breeze rustled the leaves.

The other soldiers were busy digging.

Below them the Islet River rushed downstream.

Occasionally a soldier's shovel clanged when it hit a rock.

Peering over his shoulder, Ivan had glanced at her again. Anastasia was on her knees about five yards from her family. *Don't stand up. Keep crawling,* he'd thought, wishing he could warn her directly. But she'd staggered to her feet.

And no one had noticed.

Maybe by some miracle she might—

"Hey!" a soldier had shouted. A shot rang through the woods.

Her slim form had shuddered with the impact, her arm flying up as the bullet hit her in the chest, and then her body had slumped to the ground.

Everything around Ivan had begun to spin. This was too much! Too much! He had to get out of there.

He'd put down his rifle and walked into the woods. Vaguely, Ivan knew soldiers were shouting after him. He was even aware of a bullet whistling past his ear. But he'd just kept walking.

Ivan shook off this painful memory as somewhere in town a factory whistle blew, signaling the start of the workday. These forays into the past were not welcome, and he did not succumb to them often. He was all about the future now—his future.

He walked over to the small sink and peered into the oval mirror above it. His wavy, dark brown hair was getting long, falling nearly to his shoulders. He ran his hand over the scruffy three-day stubble covering his strong chin and high cheekbones. *I should shave and get a haircut,* he considered, his straight, dark brows furrowing as he bent in closer to scrutinize his face. With a careless shrug, he decided not to bother. If their business here was successful, then he'd tend to his grooming. If not, there was no reason to care.

Suddenly the door flew open and in burst a tall, broad-shouldered, burly man in his middle twenties.

He ran his large hand across the top of his short-cropped blond hair. When he spied his friend, his clear, ice-blue eyes widened. "Come on, Ivan. We're leaving right now!" Sergei said urgently, snapping up strewn clothing as he strode around the room. "Hurry!"

CHAPTER TWO
Headline News

Nadya stretched sleepily as she shuffled down the narrow stairs from her attic bedroom above The Happy Comrades Tavern. With her eyes half-shut, she scowled at the gray morning light that filtered through a grimy window. Six in the morning was an ungodly time to start work, especially since she hadn't gotten to bed until two.

She stepped into the empty main dining area, and a misty cloud of breath formed when she yawned. An involuntary shiver ran through her, and she rubbed her arms for warmth. This morning her first chore would be to relight the fire in the room's big stone fireplace before her employer, Mrs. Zolokov, arrived. The woman hated entering a freezing building and would have an especially ratty temper all day if that happened.

Just the night before, Nadya had served and

cleaned away dishes here as the rowdy customers devoured cold borscht, rough bread, and greasy sausage or leaned against the long plank-wood bar where they downed shots of ice-cold Russian vodka, chasing them back afterward with warm beer in mugs. She'd been in Mrs. Zolokov's employ for just under a year. It was exhausting work, but it beat starving in filthy squalor on the street, something she'd done long enough to understand that it was to be avoided at all costs.

She was dressed for morning work in her faded blue shift and brown flat shoes. In the evening, when the place was crowded, Mrs. Zolokov insisted she look more presentable and had provided a flounced secondhand black skirt and a flowing, embroidered peasant-style blouse. Sometimes male customers, mostly ironworkers and miners, told her she looked attractive—though they often expressed the sentiment in cruder terms. In her own opinion she was scrawny and too pale, with dark circles under her eyes and the curse of drab, lackluster hair.

Grabbing a handful of her snarled dark blond hair—not yet swept into its usual messy updo—she breathed it in. It stank of last night's cherry-scented tobacco from cigars and pipes. And lately customers had been smoking those disgusting cigarettes, too.

Nadya would have to wash it soon, but the water from the outside pump was just so cold! Would spring never arrive?

Something lying on the wooden floor caught her

eye. It was a small, gray windup mouse that one of the customers had shown his raucous dinner companions the night before. As she was cleaning away their plates she'd heard him brag about buying the novelty in Moscow for his cat. The man probably had become so obliterated with vodka that he'd forgotten all about it. Now, after examining its lifelike tiny ears and tail, she slipped the toy mouse into her skirt pocket.

Yawning as she moved through the kitchen, Nadya went out the back door into a small yard to get some of the chopped wood from the pile. A light snow had fallen during the night and had dusted everything in sparkling white.

Three geese huddled in the goose shed while the lead male waddled out to the far end of his pen to honk angrily at her. "Oh, pipe down, you blabbermouth," Nadya scolded back. "I'll get your breakfast as soon as I can. You'll live till then." With a shudder of self-consciousness, Nadya realized she was starting to sound like Mrs. Zolokov. "I'll be back in a minute," she said to the noisy goose a bit more kindly.

Nadya gathered an armful of wood. A chilly wind made her shiver, and she hurried back into the tavern. She tossed a piece into the kitchen's wood-burning stove and dumped the rest into the main fireplace. Attempting to light a match, Nadya found that her hands were trembling from the cold. Even when she finally managed a flame, the damp wood refused to ignite.

"Newspaper," she muttered, disgruntled. In the trash can behind the bar she found old papers that customers had left behind. She lifted out the top two and stuffed them under the wood in the fireplace, and then struck her match to set the paper ablaze.

Remembering the demanding goose, Nadya went into the kitchen to retrieve the plate of stale bread she'd set aside for his meal. When she returned from feeding the geese, the paper was charred but the wood had failed to catch fire.

Mrs. Zolokov was due any minute. Glancing through the front window, Nadya saw the heavily bundled woman barreling toward the tavern; her head, covered in a flap-eared khaki-green woolen hat, was bowed against the swirls of blowing snow.

She's going to be mad, Nadya noted silently, quickly digging in her pocket for more matches.

Instead, Nadya's hand wrapped around the toy mouse.

A plan hatched. A distraction! That's what was needed!

Hurrying to the door, Nadya unbolted it and, stepping aside, wound the artificial mouse with rapid strokes.

Mrs. Zolokov turned the knob and pushed the door open.

Nadya set the toy mouse scurrying toward her boss.

"Mouse! Mouse!" the heavy woman bellowed in terror the moment she noticed the creature scurrying in circles around her feet. Hoisting her cumbersome frame onto a chair, she knocked it over as she scrambled up onto the table. "Nadya, do something! We have a mouse!"

Biting hard on her laughter, Nadya snapped up a straw broom from the side of the bar and flailed it at the toy mouse, pounding it. "I'll get you, you nasty rodent!" she cried. "Don't worry, Mrs. Z., I'll save you!" Nadya continued to whale on the toy mouse until its windup mechanism ran out. "Got it," Nadya announced proudly.

Trembling, Mrs. Zolokov made frantic shooing motions toward the kitchen with her two chubby hands. "Throw it out the back door." Then her keen, beady eyes narrowed into two suspicious black glints. "Let me see that creature. Bring it here."

As much as Nadya feared Mrs. Zolokov's rage, the comedy of the situation overcame her, and she could barely suppress a guilty smile. Dangling it by its leather tail, she presented the windup mouse.

"Why, you rotten girl!" Mrs. Zolokov cried, climbing down from the table. "I should have known this was another one of your pranks."

Nadya sang out an uncontainable hoot of hilarity. "You should have seen your face!" she cried.

Mrs. Zolokov growled with aggravation. "You are the craziest girl I've ever met."

Nadya's smile melted and she scowled darkly. "Don't say that," she snapped.

Mrs. Zolokov returned Nadya's dark expression meaningfully. "If the shoe fits. . . ."

Nadya turned away from her.

"Why is it so cold in here?" the woman demanded irritably. When Nadya explained that she couldn't get the wood to light, Mrs. Zolokov took another pile of old newspapers from the trash can. "Stick these among the logs. Haven't you learned anything by now?"

It was senseless to protest that she'd already tried it, so Nadya wordlessly approached to retrieve the papers Mrs. Zolokov held out to her. But a headline on the back page caught Mrs. Zolokov's eye. "Let me see that," she said, pulling the papers back in order to read:

**GRAND DUCHESS ANASTASIA
BELIEVED TO BE ALIVE!**

**EXILED EMPRESS OFFERS
REWARD FOR HER RETURN**

**LENIN OFFERS
COUNTER-REWARD**

Mrs. Zolokov sneered with derisive laughter. "What a fool!" she scoffed, the wattles under her double chins shaking with coldhearted merriment. "That girl is dead, dead, dead, just like the rest of the useless Imperial Family."

"Couldn't it be possible that she escaped?" Nadya questioned.

"No! You're just as daft as the empress Marie if you think so. The Bolsheviks took care to get rid of them. They'll never again be able to live in fat luxury while the Russian people starve. And I say good riddance. The only place you'll find Anastasia Nicholaevna Romanov is in a grave."

"Then why would the head of the Communist party offer a counter-reward?" Nadya argued.

Mrs. Zolokov pulled the paper closer and quickly scanned the story. "Oh, it says here that Lenin thinks it's nonsense. But if anyone does, by some miracle, come up with the girl, they are not to take her out of the country. They are to bring her in so that the comrades can handle the situation." She looked up from the paper. "You know how they'll *handle* it, of course."

"No. How?"

"They'll finish the job."

Nadya raised her hand in protest. "Don't say that. I don't like it."

"Such a silly girl," Mrs. Zolokov said, annoyed. She thrust the newspaper back at Nadya. "Here! Take this trash and put it to some good use—warming up this place."

Nadya took the paper and stuffed it, with the others, into the fireplace. Glancing at the headline regarding Anastasia, Nadya held a match to it.

CHAPTER THREE
A Girl Dressed in Goose Feathers

Ivan waved yesterday's newspaper excitedly as he and Sergei—more formally known as Count Sergei Mikhailovitch Kremnikov—walked through the streets of Yekaterinburg. Ivan was careful to side-step the noonday melting snow while Sergei hopped over snowdrifts, sometimes deliberately landing up to his knees in a high mound just for the fun of it.

"Are you paying attention to me?" Ivan impatiently demanded of his ebullient friend.

"How can I, when spring is in the air?" Sergei protested.

Ivan stretched out his arms in an expression of incredulous disbelief. "You call this spring?"

"It's coming. I can smell it," Sergei exulted.

"Look here, man. This is serious," Ivan insisted. Often it seemed to Ivan that he and his friend were a study in opposites. Ivan was slim, dark, and intense—a total contrast to the barrel-chested, blond, and sunny Sergei. Despite the five-year difference in their ages—Ivan was twenty, Sergei twenty-five—Ivan felt like the older of the two. Ivan sometimes worried that the horrors he had witnessed during his soldier service in World War I and then in the Communist Revolution had aged him prematurely, hardening him beyond his years. But then, Ivan also knew Sergei had suffered more personal losses than Ivan had. It was a mystery to him how Sergei's heart seemed so unbruised.

But Sergei frustrated Ivan when he refused to pay attention to the business at hand. It was as though he didn't really want to find an Anastasia look-alike. They'd interviewed many girls already, and Sergei would have accepted a number of them, but Ivan always found a reason to reject them. It couldn't be a girl who only approximated Anastasia's looks; the girl they chose also had to embody the lively, animated spirit of the grand duchess as Ivan had witnessed her.

If they were going to focus, Ivan would have to snap Sergei out of his infatuation with the melting snow and its promise of spring. With one sweep, Ivan brushed his unruly brown hair back from his face. "The news has made it into the paper. It's no longer our exclusive scoop. Now everyone in Russia will be searching for the grand duchess. We have to move or all the work we've done for the last two months searching for someone to play the part of

Anastasia will be wasted! We must find someone to be Anastasia!"

"Wouldn't it be wonderful if the girl lived?" Sergei suggested, his bright blue eyes shining at the idea. "You are absolutely sure Anastasia is dead?"

"We've been through this a thousand times. I saw it with my own eyes," Ivan said, a note of exasperation in his voice. Sergei was an old-time Russian loyalist from the former aristocracy. Although in this new Communist Russia it would have been dangerous to reveal his love for the czar and his family, in private Sergei was unabashedly fond of them, sometimes even swept to the point of tears when he talked about what had befallen them.

It annoyed Ivan when Sergei gushed about the old days. For his part, Ivan didn't want to think about any of it. It was over and done with. He had hardened his heart and shut the door, and now he just wanted to make some money. "She's not alive, so forget it," he said. "But if we can provide a convincing substitute to present to the grand empress, there will be a big payday for us. We can't waste time, though. Do you think we're the only two unscrupulous frauds in Russia? Anastasia look-alikes will be popping up all over when people see this story."

"Then why haven't we been able to find one in nine weeks of searching in two cities?" Sergei questioned. "Why are you being so exacting?"

"Because I saw her; these other Anastasia impostors won't be nearly as convincing as the one I can choose. When I see a girl who is a double for Anastasia, I'll know it better than most others who have only seen pictures of her. The empress will be able to spot the fakes because they won't have the movements and, you know, that certain indefinable something."

The rumor that Anastasia might be alive had first circulated among the Red soldiers, one of whom had shared it with Ivan at a tavern. Ivan came up with this plan to escape his poverty and a possible jail term. With the money, he could start a new life in a different country.

The Dowager Grand Empress Marie Feodorovna Romanov had sagely escaped to England while the Imperial Family was exiled in Siberia, and she was now living in Paris. Ivan understood that what he intended to do was fraud, but he knew what comfort it would give the old woman to have her granddaughter—reportedly her *favorite* granddaughter—restored to her. It also would lift some poor girl into a world of unimagined luxury.

This was practically a *service*, and if he could take home the 1,600,000 livres offered by the grand duchess, well, all the better. It was certainly more than he'd get from Vladimir Ilyich Lenin, the Bolshevik Communist leader. It wasn't as though he was turning some poor girl over to be murdered by the Bolsheviks just so he could collect *that* reward money—though it would have been easier. No trip to Paris, and Lenin would be easier to convince since he didn't really know the girl.

No, he and Sergei were doing the right thing, the noble thing, by finding a girl to bring to Empress Marie. The empress could afford it; he heard she lived quite well in Paris—more smuggled jewels, no doubt. Ivan's would be a scenario in which everyone came out ahead.

Sergei, too, would benefit. He had a son and a wife who had gone missing, lost in the turmoil of the Russian Communist Revolution. Sergei's search for them had exhausted the little he'd salvaged of his former fortune. The reward money would allow him to go on searching for his family. Ivan was sure it was the only reason he'd been able to talk Sergei into the plan.

"Remind me again why we're in this grim city?" Sergei said, looking around at the dirty street flanked by stores and utilitarian eateries.

"Because this is not far from where the Romanovs were assassinated," Ivan explained. "It was where the rumor began that she was alive. It might help if our girl had some knowledge of the place. Besides, we've already searched all over Moscow."

They walked toward The Happy Comrades, and Sergei looked it over with interest. "Why don't we get a bite to eat?"

"And how are you paying for this bite to eat?" Ivan questioned.

Sergei scooped out some coins from the pocket of his frayed velvet jacket. "With the money I saved by running out on our rent back at the hotel."

Ivan heartily clapped Sergei on the back. "So

that's why you rushed me out of there so fast this morning! You are a gentleman of forethought and sound economic judgment," Ivan commended him, with a sudden rise of jocular good humor. Ivan had assumed there would be no lunch for them that day, and the thought of eating immediately lifted his spirits.

They entered the plain establishment with its rough-hewn floor and uncovered tables. At least it was warm, with a fire roaring in the large stone fireplace. "Anyone here?" Sergei called into the empty room.

"Hold your horses! I'll be there in a minute!" a youthful female voice shouted from an adjacent room that appeared to be a kitchen.

Ivan looked to Sergei with sardonic laughter in his eyes. "I see we can expect hospitable service," he joked.

"Nothing but the best," Sergei agreed with a smile, seating himself at a table.

A thin young woman of about seventeen or eighteen stomped into the room. She appeared to be out of breath, her hair held back in a messy bun, her pale brow glistening with sweat. She seemed to be covered in black-and-white feathers; they stuck to her hair and out from the weave of her blue dress. The feathers fluttered from her as she approached. "We have borscht and pork sausage, beer and vodka. That's pretty much it," she told them unceremoniously, seemingly oblivious to the falling feathers.

"We'll have the sausage," Ivan ordered. "Two."

Sergei bent and lifted a feather from the floor. "I believe you dropped this," he offered with exaggerated gallantry.

A confused expression crossed the girl's face as she took it from him, but then she blasted with laughter. Realizing she was covered in the feathers, she began pulling them from her hair. "It's that goose! He got loose from the pen. I had to jump on him to get him back. He sure put up a good fight."

"Do you serve goose?" Ivan asked.

"I'd like to cook *that* one right now! But no, the owner sells them, mostly around Christmas. These geese were left over. If you haven't noticed, times are tough."

"We've noticed," Ivan muttered.

"So you still have the lucky geese that didn't get eaten over the holidays," Sergei surmised.

"Yeah, and this particular goose wasn't going to stick around until his luck ran out, either. If it were up to me, I'd set them all free just to get rid of them—they're horrible, smelly things. But that would cost me my job."

Ivan couldn't take his eyes from the girl. The movement, the body language, the facial expressions—they were all very like the Anastasia he had seen in fleeting glimpses and observed so briefly on her last terrifying day in the woods. "Do you live here in Yekaterinburg?" he asked.

"What's it to you?" she replied suspiciously.

"Just asking."

"I have a room upstairs."

"You don't live with your parents?" Ivan pressed.

The waitress tilted her head and narrowed her eyes, taking him in. "You're nosy."

Ivan waved a hand dismissively. "Interested. How old are you?" he asked her.

"I'm not sure."

"What?" Ivan cried. "How can you not be sure?"

The young woman took him in uneasily. "Maybe I'd rather not tell you."

Her defensive tone and distressed body language made Ivan sure that—incredible as it seemed—she wasn't certain of her own age. How could that be possible? What terrible past could create such a situation?

"I'll be back with your sausage," she grumbled as she left, plucking feathers from her dress as she went.

"The girl doesn't know her own age?" Sergei questioned quietly the moment the girl had disappeared into the kitchen.

"I guess not," Ivan said absently. The fact was intriguing, but Ivan couldn't focus on it at the moment. He was concentrating on a more compelling idea forming in his mind. "You're going to think I'm crazy," Ivan said to Sergei, leaning across the table with thinly suppressed excitement, "but that girl could be our Anastasia."

Sergei threw his head back and rocked with laughter. "The skinny chicken-girl there? You've got to be kidding! When she came out, I swear I expected her to cluck. And not only because of the feathers either. Did you see her legs? Chicken legs! And those manners. *Hold your horses!* Please! Very imperial, indeed."

"No, but listen to me. There's something about her."

"You're just panicking because of that news article."

"No, I'm not," Ivan protested, then paused. "Well, maybe a little. But she looks *about* the right age—whatever age she actually is doesn't matter—and she seems to be . . . you know . . . all alone."

"You don't know that," Sergei disagreed.

"Her eyes are blue."

"This is Russia!" Sergei cried. "It's the land of Slavic blue eyes. That's not enough."

"I'm telling you, she could do it," Ivan insisted.

A few minutes later, the girl returned with two plates laden with sausages, boiled potatoes, and cabbage. Ivan plied her with questions. What was her name? Where was she from? Did her family approve of her working in such a place as this? Did she have a boyfriend?

To every question she replied, "That's my business." Finally she was fed up. "You don't look like a secret-police agent but that's what you sound like," she scolded. "If you are, I haven't committed any crime."

."You're an orphan, aren't you?" Ivan said.

"Why would you think that? And besides, that's no crime."

"No, it's not a crime, but if you had a family or a home or a boyfriend, you would have said so."

The door flew open and Mrs. Zolokov bustled in, her arms wrapped around a brown bag stuffed with groceries. "Nadya, help me with these!" she shouted before realizing they had customers.

Ivan glanced up at the girl, pleased. "Ah, we have a name. Nadya." He abruptly rose from his seat and rushed to assist Mrs. Zolokov with her heavy bag. "Allow me," he said, taking it from her. The bag ripped as she transferred it to his arms, but Ivan was quick to secure the bag under his right arm, catching the contents with his left hand before they could crash to the floor.

When Ivan had settled everything on a table, he turned to Mrs. Zolokov, engaging her with his most disarming smile. "We were just talking to your delightful waitress."

"Who? Nadya? Delightful?" Mrs. Zolokov scoffed.

"In her way," Ivan insisted. "We have been asking her questions about herself, but she's very private. Wherever did you find this unique girl?"

Mrs. Zolokov cackled shrilly. "I picked her up off the street after she escaped from a mental asylum!"

CHAPTER FOUR
An Insane Offer

Mortified, Nadya fled through the kitchen and out the back door. The voracious geese cried out to her, but she ran past them and settled on a broken stone wall that wound down a slope leading to the Islet River. She shivered and wrapped her arms tightly around her slim frame as tears poured down her cheeks.

What did she care what those men thought of her? But Mrs. Zolokov's words had been so embarrassing! Every time the horrible woman joked around about her being from the asylum, she wanted to die! It was humiliating.

If ever any young man seemed interested in her—and occasionally one who seemed nice paid her special attention—Mrs. Zolokov would say in a thundering voice, "Leave her alone. You don't want to be mixed up with a mental patient." And that would be the end of that!

But sometimes Nadya really did feel that she was going insane. Crazy nightmares plagued her, keeping her in a sleepless fog for many days.

Of her past, all she knew from her own experience was that she'd spent time in the Yekaterinburg Mental Asylum. Shortly before the Bolsheviks took over the asylum, there was a fire and all the asylum's records were lost. Anyone with a known relative was sent home. Others like her who had untraceable families were simply turned out.

At the asylum, no one could quite recall how or when Nadya had arrived, because there was such a high turnover of personnel. Some said the police had left her there because she had been found wandering the streets alone and confused. Others thought they remembered that her parents had brought her in over a year earlier. The fact that Nadya couldn't remember any of her life before the asylum was simply a manifestation of her mental illness; hysterical amnesia, the bald psychiatrist had pronounced. He was one of many doctors that had come and gone from the asylum.

When the asylum closed, Nadya had roamed the streets, begging for food, sleeping in barns and old sheds. Finally, she'd collapsed on the street here in Yekaterinburg where Mrs. Zolokov had found her. She'd recognized a source of nearly free labor when she saw one.

Nadya rubbed her forehead and shivered. Mostly she tried to pay attention to her chores and keep her mind as clear as possible. She didn't need someone like that man to come stir things up with intrusive questions about her life. His probing had been as upsetting as Mrs. Zolokov's remark.

Something warm enfolded her from behind. It was a velvet jacket, and she looked up to see the blond customer from inside—the nice one, not his probing, arrogant friend with the over-intense dark eyes. "You were shivering," he said, sitting on the wall beside her.

Nadya wiped her eyes, embarrassed by her tears. "It's all right. I'm all right," she insisted. "Take back your jacket, please."

"No, no, you keep it. It's the least I can do after we have all been so boorish to you. Nadya, let me introduce myself. My name is Sergei. My friend Ivan and I are from Moscow."

Nadya nodded. "Why was your friend asking so many questions?" she asked, feeling soothed by the man's gentle tone.

"Here is the thing. My friend Ivan and I are private detectives. Do you know what that is?" She shook her head. She'd never heard the words. "We are like the secret police, only we work privately for individual clients," he explained.

"What do you want with me? I told you—I haven't done anything wrong."

Nadya listened in amazement to the explanation he gave her. He and Ivan had been contacted by an elderly woman, a minor countess living in exile in

Paris. She was a White Russian—a name given to the many members of the aristocracy who had fled Russia during the revolution rather than be killed by the Bolsheviks. She'd wanted to pick up her granddaughter from a mental asylum in Yekaterinburg, but the urgency of her leaving made it impossible. So she had asked Ivan and Sergei to come find her.

"She offered you money to do this?" Nadya asked.

Sergei shrugged. "The old woman hinted at some payment, but we're not interested in that. We only want to help. We loyalists must stick together."

Nadya studied him. He was in his mid-twenties, probably several years older than the other one. He had a somewhat bland, flat, but pleasant face with pale eyes. He appeared trustworthy, almost brotherly.

"Mrs. Zolokov told you the truth. I was in a mental asylum before I came to work for her," she told him plainly, without emotion. That was how it was and he should know it.

"How are you feeling these days?" Sergei asked her.

"A little shaky sometimes," she admitted.

"Maybe you will feel better when you get out of here," he suggested with equanimity. "You simply might need to go home."

Tears sprang to her eyes.

You simply might need to go home.

Home. Was there such a place for her? It sounded too good to be true.

"Please don't cry," Sergei said with a note of male panic at the threat of tears. "I didn't mean to upset you."

It was too late even to attempt to hold back. Great surges flooded Nadya's eyes. She drew in gulps of cold air that shook her slim shoulders and rushed out in great sobs. Nadya wanted to explain to him why she was so overcome, but how could she even begin to put into words the awful loneliness she lived with every day? The idea that she had a grandmother somewhere, one who was searching for her—it was too much, too wonderful to be real.

"There, there." Sergei comforted her, wrapping an arm soothingly around Nadya's heaving shoulders. "I can see it's been hard."

Those rare words of compassion were enough to set her off crying even more violently.

No one *ever* saw how difficult Nadya's life was, because her pride didn't allow it. What if others saw and didn't care? What if she let them in to her pain and they took advantage? She joked and acted tough because it seemed more dignified than being pitiful and needy. Even now she felt an impulse, one born of habit, to shrug away Sergei's arm and say she was fine, he needn't bother, she'd manage—but she didn't do it. This release of pent-up, driven-down sorrow was so long overdue that she couldn't stop it.

"Are you crying because you *want* to meet your grandmother or because you don't?" Sergei asked cautiously.

"I want to, but I'm scared," she admitted.

"Scared of what?"

"Lots of things. I don't know you, and your friend is unpleasant. I didn't like the way he looked at me; it was like he was picking me apart."

"Ivan's all right, just intense. He had a hard time during The Revolution. If you come with us, I swear we'll treat you like a little sister. You have my word."

"You swear on your mother?"

"I swear on my mother."

"Look at me," she said, wiping her swollen eyes again and rubbing her running nose with her sleeve. "I'm no prize! What if my grandmother hates me?"

"You're her granddaughter. How can she hate you?"

"My parents obviously hated me. They abandoned me at a lunatic asylum!"

"That's probably not so! Perhaps it was for your own good. Maybe they did it to protect you from the Bolsheviks," Sergei suggested.

Nadya had never thought of that before. "You mean I might *not* be crazy?"

"You don't look crazy to me," Sergei allowed. "I suppose we'll find out," he added with just a touch of worry in his voice. "But even if it's so, your grandmother has the means to get you to competent doctors who can help you if you need. And besides, we're all feeling a little nuts these days. Since The Revolution all our lives have been turned upside down. The old stability has been swept away. Maybe it will be for the better—who knows?—but for now, it feels as though the whole world's gone mad."

"It does seem that way," Nadya said, a small smile playing at the corners of her lips. "If I'm crazy, I do have a lot of company."

Sergei's shoulders shook with laughter. "Absolutely." He gazed at her warmly. "Then you're up for the trip?"

Nadya stood and nodded.

"Excellent!" Sergei cried. "A most excellent decision!"

Nadya handed Sergei back his velvet jacket and said she would meet him and Ivan behind the tavern after she'd gathered her things. Then she hurried up the back steps to her room so she wouldn't encounter Mrs. Zolokov.

The moment she was out of Sergei's comforting presence, though, Nadya's confidence in this plan leaked away. She was running off with two strangers. If these two turned out to be unsavory characters, she would have no one to blame but herself.

Nadya paced the tiny room. *What to do? What to do?*

She instinctively trusted Sergei, but if he were so wonderful, then what was he doing keeping company with the other one, Ivan? Ivan put her on guard. He was wolfish, too alert and harsh. He asked questions in a way she didn't appreciate, like an interrogator.

Nadya sat on the corner of her bed, which creaked under the weight of her slim body. She gazed at the worn and sagging floor, the splintered beams, the frayed rug and grimy, cracked window. Look how she was living! Was hers even a life worth protecting? Before Sergei and Ivan, she had had not a clue how to escape it. She might marry the first oaf who offered. Maybe he would be such a miserable dunce of a man that he wouldn't care that she couldn't remember most of her life story.

Nadya laughed bleakly. Some high aspirations she had, hoping to marry some dope too dense to care if he was marrying a lunatic.

Nadya dumped the straw stuffing from her pillowcase, pulling out the last bits with her hand. She could make it work as a satchel for her things.

"Okay, here we go," she muttered aloud. From under the bed, she began gathering her few possessions: the peasant blouse, the black flounced skirt, an old ripped petticoat, and her black shoes, which were slightly better than the ones she wore now. Onto the center of the bed went a hairbrush and some underwear she'd bought with her meager pay.

Was there anything else?

Nadya picked up a small cloth doll that sat on her windowsill. The smiling toy had a merry expression stitched on his face. Its vivid blue eyes were two buttons. It had been in the pocket of her skirt when she'd awakened at the asylum. The doll had been badly tattered; she recalled that its head was nearly off until a kind nurse at the asylum had repaired it for her.

She had no need for the worn plaything now. Her new companions would think it childish if they saw her with a doll, and she didn't want that. "Here's where we part company," she told the doll tenderly. "I'm too old for dolls."

Nadya would need a coat—too bad she didn't own one. Mrs. Zolokov also owed her over a week's pay. Nadya pulled her blanket from the bed and threw it around her shoulders like a big cape. The pay she was not going to collect was worth more than this moth-eaten wool.

"Okay. Okay," she muttered. "Are you really going through with this, you crazy girl?" There could be no doubt—if she left with them it would mean she really was insane.

Maybe not insane, but certainly reckless!

But who cared? No one!

And that was the whole point. If somewhere in the world there was a grandmother who *did* care, it was worth any chance, every chance.

Nadya tied the ends of the pillowcase together, then used the knotted middle as a handle. With her blanket over her shoulders and clutching her home-made satchel, Nadya stepped outside her room. Below, at the bottom of the stairs, Sergei and Ivan waited. Sergei waved and Ivan peered up the stairs, scowling, as though still studying her like some kind of specimen.

Nadya ducked back inside, heart pounding, scared. Was she really going to go through with this?

She turned to the doll on the windowsill. "What do you think, my little friend?" Nadya asked it. "Is what I'm about to do insane?"

Nadya had developed the habit of bouncing

her ideas, concerns, and worries off of the doll. The smiling face had offered her comfort and companionship through many lonely, frightening times— unfortunately, though, it could not really offer her advice and she knew it.

"You're right," Nadya said, addressing the doll as though it had answered her. "Staying here will get me nowhere. I might as well take this chance and hope for the best."

Nadya snapped the doll off the windowsill. "What was I thinking?" she said. "I could never leave you behind, my little friend." Maybe her attachment to the doll *was* childish, but she didn't care. She loved it too much to leave it behind. Nadya stuffed the doll into the pillowcase satchel—an old friend to bring along for luck!

She pushed the door open again. *Here we go.*

CHAPTER FIVE
A Spy at the Station

As they walked along at a brisk pace toward the Trans-Siberian Railroad station, Ivan stole darting glances at Nadya. He did not dare to stare at her as long as he would have liked. Ivan wanted to examine every inch of her again and again to assure himself that his first impression had been correct. He suspected that, under all her messiness, Nadya might be pretty. He hoped so. Anastasia had been very pretty, as he recalled.

Everything was riding on this now.

But whenever Nadya caught Ivan gazing at her for overlong, she glared at him fiercely and hunched her shoulders defensively. It made her appear less like a grand duchess than anyone on earth and shook his confidence about their choice. Did Nadya really resemble Anastasia as strongly as he'd thought at first sight?

Had Sergei been right in saying that Ivan was panicking and jumping at the nearest girl he found to present as Anastasia?

Possibly.

Ivan and Sergei were stuck with her now, though, and he had to make the best of it. Once they got that filthy hair washed and put her in some decent clothing, he'd have a better idea of what he was working with.

Ivan was relying on such brief snaps of memory for all this: the blithe spirit in a white sailor-style frock seen at a distance dancing down the garden paths of The House of Special Purpose, a note of melodic laughter carried on a summer breeze, a half-dead adolescent dragging herself from a grave site, the nightmares—surely he saw her again and again in the nightmares.

The large sign for the railroad station came into view. The sidewalks grew more crowded the closer they got, and it suddenly made Ivan conscious of Nadya's ragged appearance. Passersby cast furtive, disapproving glances her way. Ivan shrugged off his woolen jacket and offered it to her. "Put this on."

"I'm not cold," she declined.

"You look like a beggar in that blanket," Ivan argued.

Nadya reared back, insulted. "You're no prize either. I don't want your smelly jacket."

Sergei took the coat from Ivan, and then gently unwrapped the blanket from Nadya's shoulders.

"Take his old thing for now," he insisted in a voice that apparently soothed her. "I'll carry the blanket and you can use it again when you sleep on the train."

Nodding, Nadya slipped into the jacket that Sergei held out for her.

How well he manages her! Sergei is like that with everyone, though, Ivan thought. *He is the kind of aristocrat who is truly noble.*

Ivan had been surprised that Sergei had never been arrested by the Bolsheviks, who persecuted all the former nobility. It seemed so clear from his manner that he had once been *Count* Sergei Mikhailovitch Kremnikov. He'd survived simply by walking away from everything he'd once had, abandoning it all to the Bolsheviks.

Now Sergei fell into step with Ivan, speaking to him in lowered tones so Nadya wouldn't hear. "Where are we going, by the way?"

"Paris, of course," Ivan answered.

"Do we even know how to get to Paris?" Sergei asked.

"Of course I do," Ivan replied. "You know I've been planning this for months."

"Shouldn't we spruce up the, er, *duchess*, before we go?" Sergei pointed out.

"It's a long trip, especially with no money for a ship or train ticket. We can work with her along the way." Again, Ivan glanced at Nadya trudging along in his too-big-for-her jacket. It might be a blessing that the journey would be so long. Turning her into a believable grand duchess was going to take some doing.

They walked into the station and were greeted by a busy room full of people. The train station was not as grand as the one in Moscow, but it was still large, with twenty-foot tin ceilings that caused the many voices within to echo, amplifying the din. "Last car, last minute?" Ivan checked with Sergei.

"Last car, last minute," Sergei confirmed. "We'll take it as far west as we can." This was their usual strategy for traveling without the benefit of tickets. Once the train sounded its departure whistle, the conductors left their positions on the platform between trains where they checked the tickets of the boarding passengers. Sergei and Ivan would then hop on. They had to be fast, because it was only a minute or two after the whistle blast before the train would begin to move.

"Should we inform her highness of the train boarding plan?" Ivan asked.

"I don't think so. It might undermine her already—shall we say—*fragile* confidence in us," Sergei replied.

"Good point," Ivan agreed. "I don't think she trusts us at all, especially not me. We'll just stall until the last possible moment."

They saw a sign for a train heading to Moscow. With a nod, Sergei ushered Nadya toward it. "Our first stop on the way to Paris," Sergei explained.

Before they got to the track, Ivan suggested they

use the public toilet facilities that the train station offered. It seemed like a good idea and would cause some natural delay.

Directing Nadya toward the room marked for females—the Bolsheviks had changed all signs from LADIES and GENTLEMEN to the more proletariat-friendly MEN and WOMEN—Ivan and Sergei went into the men's restroom.

As they washed in the cold water at the sinks, Sergei explained that he had told Nadya she might be the granddaughter of some minor White Russian countess in exile. "I feared that our real intention might frighten her off," he said.

"It probably would," Ivan agreed. "How did you get her to think she might be the granddaughter of a countess, though? Is that even possible to her?"

Sergei told Ivan about Nadya's amnesia. "Anything's possible," Sergei suggested. "Since the truth of her birth parents is unknown, and may never be known, she could be from anywhere."

"I've never seen Paris. Have you?" Ivan asked as he dried his hands.

"I have," Sergei divulged. "You'll love it—or you'll hate it, depending on how you feel about priceless art, beautiful women, and fabulous food."

"It sounds very *bourgeois*," Ivan noted.

"It is not an accident that the word to describe a life of comfort is French," Sergei pointed out. "And to think that their revolution took place over a hundred years before ours did."

"I try to no longer have opinions about anything political or otherwise," Ivan remarked.

"You are a cynic," Sergei said.

"I am disgusted with life and weary to the bone, that's all," Ivan countered.

"Weary at twenty?" Sergei questioned doubtfully.

"Is that all I am?" Ivan asked as they left the bathroom. "I thought I was one hundred and twenty."

Sergei stopped before they left the bathroom. "I think I might have been wrong not to tell Nadya that we want her to pose as Anastasia. I don't feel right about it."

"I disagree. She might not have come if she knew we were involving her in a fraud. Why don't we tell her we believe she is Anastasia? Why not? She has no memory anyway. How could she argue?"

"I don't know," Sergei said warily.

"We'll wait until we get on the train. That way she can't bolt," Ivan insisted.

"But is it right to make her believe she's someone she's not?" Sergei questioned.

"Think of it this way: If she's going to live the rest of her days as Grand Duchess Anastasia, isn't it better if she believes that's who she really is?"

"I suppose," Sergei agreed, following Ivan out the door.

Nadya rushed to them the moment they stepped into the station. Grabbing the lapel of Sergei's jacket, she spoke rapidly to him. "A man behind that pillar was spying on me."

"Spying?" Ivan asked.

"Yes!" she cried. "He was very thin with a horrible scar across his face. He wore a long dark coat. Every time I looked at him, he ducked back behind the pillar."

"Is he there now?" Sergei asked, his eyes darting around the station.

"I don't know," Nadya answered.

"Have you ever seen him before?" Ivan asked, looking from left to right.

"At first I thought he looked familiar, but I couldn't recall a name or where I might know him from. I suppose I was mistaken," Nadya replied.

"Wait here," Ivan said. Making a wide loop around the station at a jog, he came up behind the pillar. No one was there. He surveyed the station for a man fitting Nadya's description but found no one.

Had there been a man or was this some paranoid delusion?

He'd have to be watchful for this sort of thing. Mrs. Zolokov had warned them that Nadya was from an insane asylum, after all.

CHAPTER SIX
An Imperial Dream

Nadya settled into her seat by the window and watched the countryside roll by. The compartment they were in was extremely pleasant. They'd nearly missed their train because Sergei and Ivan had insisted on searching for the scarred man until the very last second. They'd had to run and jump on the train as it was already beginning to move. And then it took forever for them to find this compartment.

But now that they were settled, Nadya hoped they had left that creep from the station behind. Sergei seemed to believe her, but Nadya suspected that Ivan thought she was making it up or was just acting crazy. She could tell he was not the trusting sort, and Mrs. Zolokov's remarks had made him wary of her.

Sergei had left the compartment, saying he needed to check into something regarding their tickets. She wondered when he'd even had time to buy them. She hadn't seen him do it; maybe he'd purchased the tickets while she was in the bathroom.

She looked over at Ivan across the way, his eyes shut and his head hung down, arms crossed and long legs stretched out on the empty seat beside him. There was no denying that he was very handsome—in a ragged, unkempt way, of course. If he wasn't so rude and off-putting, she might even be attracted to him.

Don't even think it! she scolded herself. *To fall for Ivan would be the worst mistake you could make.* At the tavern she'd seen plenty of young women involved with men who treated them rudely—it was painful to watch.

Leaning closer to the window, Nadya gazed out. The train rocked gently while the sunlight threw a blanket of warmth over her. Soon Nadya's temple rested on the glass as her eyes drifted shut.

The dreams that crowded her sleeping mind were erratic. One moment she was swirling at a grand ball, and in the next she was learning to speak French. Nadya would awaken, look out as the snowy landscape moved past, shift in her seat, and fall back to sleep, only to plunge once again into the shadowy world of elusive dreams.

Nadya awoke once to see a hazy sunset over the mountains. Sergei was talking quietly to a conductor. "My friend is sleeping on a coat containing our tickets," he said, pointing to the slumbering Ivan across from her. "He's exhausted. Can we let him sleep a while longer?"

As the conductor consented to this, Nadya shifted once more, dimly aware of the conversation, and then returned to her dreams.

Nadya is still in the train compartment, but it has somehow grown more lavish, with ornate gold trim on both the walls and seats. They are going around a mountainside. Below them is a very dark sea. "Is the ocean filled with ink?" she asks a regal man in a military uniform who comes into the compartment. He has a big mustache and is very, very tall. But then Nadya realizes that he is not as tall as she'd first thought. It is she who has grown smaller.

She vaguely recognizes that the man is Czar Nicholas, the ruler of Russia.

"The sea is not filled with ink," he says kindly. "You have been sleeping since St. Petersburg. We will soon be to Livadia."

"I have a mouse in my pocket," she tells him. "I scared Mrs. Zolokov with it. Are you proud of me?"

Czar Nicholas pets her hair. "Shvizbik," he says fondly.

Nadya looks out the window again and sees a train that is an exact duplicate of the one they are on. "Why are there two trains?" she asks.

"To fool anyone who would try to hurt us," the tall man replies.

"Who would want to hurt us?" she asks. But before he can answer she hears gunfire! Bullets crash through the window.

She screams as loudly as she can. If she can scream louder than the noise, she won't have to hear it!

∽   ∽   ∽

"Nadya! Nadya! Wake up!" Sergei was shaking her awake.

"What's the matter with her?" Ivan demanded. "Make her stop screaming!"

"Shh! Shh!" Sergei hushed her urgently. "Nadya! Snap out of it!"

"Those gunshots! Who shot at us?" she asked frantically as she came awake. Nadya was back in the simple coach compartment.

"I was dreaming again," she realized. "One of my nightmares."

"Tell us about it," Sergei urged.

"It was strange. The czar of Russia, Nicholas, was there. I know him from photos, but in the dream it seemed perfectly natural that I could speak with him."

"That's dreams for you," Ivan remarked.

Nadya nodded. "We were in a train passing by a sea filled with black ink."

"The Black Sea!" Sergei cried excitedly. "I have read books by a psychologist named Freud. He believes that our dreams are not always direct, but instead they speak to us in a complex language of symbols and word games."

"So you think that a sea of black ink is the Black Sea?" Ivan questioned.

"Of course it is," Sergei insisted. "Nadya, can you recall ever being there?"

"I told you, I can't remember. Right now I'm not even sure where the Black Sea is."

"Many wealthy Russians had summer homes in the mountains of the Crimea, overlooking the Black Sea," Sergei explained. "The Imperial Family even had a place there. See? This is proof that your family was aristocratic."

Ivan looked at him doubtfully. "A dream about ink isn't proof of anything," he disagreed.

"I thought you believed I really could be this girl you are looking for," Nadya said, challenging him with an edge of annoyance in her voice. "Have you changed your mind about me?"

"What I believe won't matter if we can't convince the countess that you are her lost granddaughter," he replied.

"Convince her?" Nadya asked. "Won't she recognize me?"

"You were younger when she last saw you," Sergei reminded Nadya. "I'm sure you've changed a great deal. She may question whether we've found the right girl."

"How can we convince her?" Nadya asked. "I've told you I have no memory."

Sergei sat down beside her. "We will give you memories based on what we know of this girl's life."

"What was my name?" Nadya wanted to know.

Ivan and Sergei exchanged questioning glances. Nadya noticed and felt confused. What was going on? Didn't they know her name? And if not, why not?

"Anna," Ivan said.

"Anna what?"

Again, Nadya sensed their discomfort. They looked at one another uneasily but did not answer.

"What is it you are not telling me?" Nadya demanded. "I may have no memory, but I'm not stupid. Something's going on. Why won't you tell me the girl's name?"

Sergei took hold of Nadya's hand and gazed into her eyes. Nadya shifted away from him a bit. A feeling of ominous dread welled within her. Whatever information he was about to impart had filled him with a new solemnity, and it frightened her. "What?" She pressed him to speak.

Ivan leaned in. "Nadya, we believe you may be the grand duchess Anastasia Romanov."

Wide-eyed, Nadya looked incredulously from one to the other. Then she got it. "He's joking, correct?" She checked with Sergei, suddenly sure Ivan had to be mocking her.

Sergei shook his head. "We're very serious."

A wild bark of laughter rose from inside her. "And they say *I'm* insane!" she cried. "You two are totally out of your minds!"

This was awful—she'd run off with two lunatics! Though if it had been happening to someone else, she'd think it was hilarious.

Agitated, she got up and began to pace. "I should have known this was too good to be true. I must have been the biggest idiot on earth to have thought that you two were going to whisk me out of my miserable existence into some fairy tale. And now, here I am in a worse predicament than I had been in back at The Happy Comrades."

It was all just ridiculous, really, and she began to laugh so hard that she fell over onto the empty seat beside Ivan and let a hysterical fit of giggles rock her.

"Nadya, stop," Ivan implored. "Stop and listen."

"I can't stop," she insisted through outbursts of laughter. "It's all too funny. If I'm Anastasia, who are you? Napoleon?" She pointed to Sergei. "I suppose he's Peter the Great!"

Sergei took hold of each of her hands. The gentle but firm gesture calmed her to a breathless panting. "Surely you see how funny all this is," she said.

"Why *couldn't* you be Anastasia?" Sergei asked without any hint of levity.

"Because she's dead, for one thing."

"Her grandmother doesn't think so," Ivan countered. "She may have received reports that we don't know about. She's still well-connected throughout Russia."

"Is that so?" Nadya questioned skeptically. "Her Imperial Highness, the Dowager Grand Empress Marie Feodorovna Romanov, *personally* sought out you two to find Anastasia?"

"No, not *personally*," Sergei admitted sheepishly. "But we received information that—"

"I saw it in the newspaper too," she shouted, cutting Sergei off as the memory came roaring back to her. "Mrs. Zolokov had me use the article as a fire starter."

Clutching her forehead, she closed her eyes in

a futile attempt to block out everything. Oh, what giant mess had she gotten herself into?

"Mrs. Zolokov doesn't have the inside information that I have," Ivan said seriously.

The earnest sincerity of his tone caught Nadya by surprise. It was a note she hadn't heard from him before. But she refused to let on that he had her attention, and she kept her eyes clenched shut.

"Look at me, Nadya. I'm telling you the truth," Ivan insisted. "We have inside information."

Nadya opened one eye just a little. "Oh yes?" she said. "And what information is that?"

CHAPTER SEVEN
Fast Thinking

"I served as a stable boy at the Peterhof Palace," Ivan lied with a certainty he hoped was convincing. "I drove along with my father, the head coachman to the Imperial Family."

There was an element of truth in this fabrication. In reality he'd *visited* the grand palace, with its many fountains and statues built by Peter the Great. He'd gone with his father, who had sharpened kitchen utensils and repaired broken blades and handles. Though he never laid eyes on any member of the Imperial Family back then, he had once bumped into the czarina Alexandra's sinister adviser, the supposed "holy man" Father Grigory Rasputin.

Rasputin was a big, powerfully built figure with a long, ragged black beard. He often dressed in a dirty black cassock. Ivan vividly recalled his revulsion at the bad energy, not to mention the foul odor—a mix of garlic and days-old sweat—emanating from him.

"Anastasia and I were friends." Ivan went on lying. "We played together."

He paused to see how she accepted this news. Her eyes were narrowed suspiciously. He would have to progress with care. Nadya reminded him of a deer whose ears were tuned to the footfall of hunters in the forest. One misstep along the path and she'd be on to him.

Ivan was now having doubts about the wisdom of lying to her. Why not tell her they planned to swindle the old dame out of her money by providing a plausible substitute for her dead granddaughter? Maybe Nadya would go for it and play along willingly. What would she have to lose?

But Ivan always lived by his instincts, and they were telling him that this girl wouldn't be part of a scam, no matter how advantageous it might prove to her. Despite Nadya's rough appearance and all the hard knocks she must have taken, there was something intrinsically fresh and straightforward about her. The only way this was going to work was if she believed it. There was so much to be gained for everyone if Nadya only would believe she was Anastasia Romanov: for her, it was a family member to take her in and love her, not to mention a life of luxury; for Sergei and Ivan, it was the reward money; for the grand duchess, it was the return of her granddaughter. It was a worthy enterprise, a good deed, but it had to be done carefully.

"Anastasia and I were friends, and so that is why I have made it my cause to search for her," he continued. "If I can find her and restore the lost duchess to her rightful place, that is a debt I owe to our friendship, and I am glad to do it."

Those squinting eyes still bore into him. "You and I were friends?"

"Dear friends," he confirmed.

"Just why are you so certain I am your dear friend? Why don't you accept that she is dead when soldiers have sworn that they shot her?"

"I have met people who have said they saw Anastasia wandering in the Ural Mountains days after the assassination." This was true. These rumors had circulated for the last year, though they were based on unsubstantiated sightings. Anastasia had not been an unusual-looking girl: blond, very pretty, of medium height and build. Certainly there were many other fair-haired, attractive girls in Russia who could have been mistaken for the youngest grand duchess.

The silhouette of a conductor appeared behind the frosted glass of the compartment door. "Pretend you're asleep!" Sergei hissed to Ivan and Nadya in a whisper. "Now!"

They all slumped back in their seats. Ivan feigned a low snore as the conductor opened the door and called for tickets. Usually the conductor went away, giving them time to move to another compartment or, if none was available, to change trains at the next stop.

Instead, the conductor opened their compartment door and called more insistently, "Tickets."

Sergei shushed him, pretending to awaken suddenly. "My sister is very sick and has just now fallen asleep."

"Sorry," the conductor replied in a whisper. "Tickets, please."

Sergei patted his pockets as if searching for something. "I was sure I had them in here. Er . . . in my overcoat, perhaps . . . now I *just* saw that overcoat. . . ."

With his eyes still shut, Ivan struggled to come up with a plan to aid the stammering Sergei.

Nadya suddenly gave a strangled cry that made Ivan's eyes snap. She flailed her arms like a person drowning. "Air! I can't breathe! My throat—it's closing!"

She staggered across the compartment, and then collapsed heavily onto the conductor, who jumped back. "Sir, your sister! What's wrong with her?"

"Is there a doctor on board?" Ivan asked.

"Yes, yes there is," the conductor said, handing off Nadya's slumped form to Sergei. "I'll get him at once."

The moment the conductor left, Nadya's eyes opened. "Well, I got rid of him. Now what do we do?" she asked.

Ivan stepped back, shocked. He'd completely believed her throat was closing. "You're all right?" he asked.

"Yes, fine. But clearly we have no tickets. They arrest people for riding the train without tickets, you know."

Sergei set her down gently onto the seat and

stepped into the corridor. "I thought we could give them the slip for a few more stations," he murmured.

"She's right," Ivan agreed. "We have to get off at the next station."

"We have to get off now," Sergei corrected him, his eyes locked on someone coming down the hallway toward them.

"Now?" Ivan and Nadya cried at the same time.

"The conductor is returning with a doctor and a police officer," Sergei reported urgently.

Nadya snapped up her pillowcase bundle as Ivan hurried her out of the compartment. They moved out quickly to the platform of the last car. All around them were rolling hills dotted with patches of snow.

Ivan glanced over his shoulder and saw the conductor rushing toward them with the policeman. Instinctively, he grabbed Nadya's hand. She didn't shy away but gripped his hand tightly.

"One, two, three!" he counted. On three, they leapt together from the moving train.

Ivan's shoulder hit the ground with a painful thud, and the next thing he knew, he was rolling down a slope holding Nadya tightly against him. She held him around the waist as they rolled over and over down the hill until they landed hard, crashing into a shallow creek. Sergei was several yards away from them, sitting in the running water.

Nadya was shaking with laughter. It wasn't like the near-hysteria that had seized her before—this was simple exhilaration. "Whew! What a ride!" she cried happily and threw her head back to continue laughing.

Her laughter was so contagious that it made Ivan laugh also. He realized he was doing something he hadn't done for over a year. How wonderful it felt to explode with uproarious mirth! It was as though a spark, long dead in him, had been unexpectedly rekindled.

CHAPTER EIGHT
Moving Closer, Stepping Back

Sergei warmed his hands by the fire they had made that evening. He chuckled to himself as he gazed into the crackling blaze. What an adventure it had been so far!

Across from him, Ivan and Nadya had curled up close to the warmth of the fire and played a desultory game with the soggy deck of cards that—along with a few coins—had been in Sergei's pocket when they had jumped from the train. Ivan and Nadya had spoken only about the cards and had barely looked at each other.

Nadya still wore Ivan's coat, though, since she'd left her old wool blanket on the train. Now her paltry belongings, which had been soaked in the creek, were spread out by the fire: some well-worn clothing and a rag doll. Seeing the doll touched Sergei. It was such a tender, childish item for her to have brought along—a stark contrast to the tough face she showed to the world.

She was an interesting girl, at once hard and soft. With a good scrubbing and a few extra pounds on her, she'd be pretty, though he had no idea how they'd unsnarl that squirrel's nest of hair on her head.

Could he really teach this scruffy creature imperial ways? She was quick-witted and obviously had a good sense of humor, but she didn't appear to have an ounce of style. Sergei had assumed they'd select a girl of some breeding for the job, not a pub waitress who was one step above a scullery maid. It wasn't that Sergei didn't like her—he did. But Nadya was so clearly ill-equipped for this assignment.

From the other side of the fire, he couldn't hear what Ivan was muttering to Nadya, but it was making her smile. Unexpectedly, a pang of loss shot through him. Something in Nadya's smile reminded him of Elana, his wife.

When Sergei had heard that the Bolsheviks were heading toward his estate, he'd sent Elana and their one-year-old son Peter away to stay with his aunt in Sweden. Because the Bolsheviks had kept Sergei a prisoner while they took over his estate, it was weeks before he was allowed to write to his aunt to inquire after his wife and son. When the answering letter had finally reached him, the news was devastating: they had never arrived.

In the last year and a half, Sergei had walked all the roads they might have taken and had turned up not a single clue as to their whereabouts. Now he was simply out of ideas as to where his family might be and devoid of the funds it would require to continue the search.

That was why he'd agreed to this plan despite his better judgment. If it were a way to find Elana and Peter, Sergei would agree to nearly anything.

Nadya laughed again at something Ivan said. She really did have the most infectious laugh, and it made Sergei smile. He was glad she was no longer thinking about the frightening man she'd seen at the station. Remembering how scared she'd been made Sergei think of someone he hadn't thought about in a long, long time: a short man with a horrible twisted scar.

At the moment, Sergei couldn't recall the man's name, but he'd seen him once or twice when attending public events at the palace. The man had always been at Rasputin's side. Rasputin had been assassinated by members of the aristocracy, but Sergei had never learned what had become of his scarred assistant. Was it possible that he was now a member of the Secret Police? It could be. A twisted, secretive little man like that would be just the type to sell his services to the highest bidder. But why would he be following them? Was he looking to bring in Ivan as a deserter from the army?

Or might he be tracking them because they really had the grand duchess Anastasia with them?

Sergei got up and stretched, trying to shake the

worrisome thoughts from his head. He watched Nadya concentrating on her hand of cards as the golden glow from the fire played over her face. Seen in this soft light, her expression so serious and her eyes so focused on her card game, Sergei saw how delicate Nadya was, how refined—even regal—a profile she had.

Ivan had said it was impossible that Anastasia could live, and while Sergei wanted to believe him ...

At the very least, Ivan had selected well. Despite his first impressions, Sergei now was convinced that, with some work, Nadya would make a very believable grand duchess.

"I'm going to sleep," Sergei announced.

"Good night, Sergei," Ivan and Nadya both murmured, their voices tumbling over each other.

Nadya glanced up from her cards. "Sleep well."

"Thanks. And you, as well," he replied with a gentle smile. This spirited, lovely girl had become like a younger sister to him. He couldn't let anything bad happen to her.

The next day Ivan, Sergei, and Nadya covered over ten miles thanks to a farmer who gave them a ride in the back of the hay wagon he was taking to market. While Ivan napped, Nadya mischievously buried him in hay, and then awoke him by tickling his nose with straw. Sergei had to chuckle as, still asleep, Ivan tried to bat away the straw as if it were a pestering bug. Ivan squirmed in his sleep, trying to move his arms, which were buried under the hay.

Nadya shrieked with laughter when Ivan awoke and realized his predicament. With a powerful lunge forward, Ivan broke free from under the hay and immediately began showering straw on Nadya. She howled as she swatted him away with one hand and grabbed handfuls of hay to retaliate with the other hand. In the end, they both lay in the truck covered in hay and smiling. Sergei chuckled and shook his head good-naturedly. It was good to see they were no longer scowling at each other.

They unloaded wrapped bales of hay for the farmer and picked up a few coins for a meager lunch of cheese and bread that they ate by a stream. The day after that, an iceman let them help him deliver blocks of frozen water to his customers to cool their iceboxes. It was backbreaking work, but Nadya kept it lively by constantly dropping ice shavings down the back of Ivan's shirt, always when he least expected it. Sergei roared with laughter at the sight of Ivan wriggling to fish out the ice, and then running after Nadya with ice shavings of his own, trying—sometimes successfully—to get her back.

This work on the ice truck moved them forward another eight miles, and the iceman bought them supper as recompense for their labor.

On the third day they met a traveling salesman who wanted company in his British roadster. "This is the new Russia of the working class. Workers need uniforms and uniforms require buttons, which is where I come in," he told Sergei, who was seated in the front beside him.

"How is that?" Sergei asked him.

"I sell buttons! It's a great time to be in the button business. By this time next year, I'll be rich!"

"Excuse my saying so, but isn't the whole idea of the new Bolshevik Russia that no one is richer than anyone else?" Ivan pointed out from the backseat.

The salesman gave a sputtering laugh. "That will blow over soon enough. It goes against human nature. People are naturally competitive. They will always strive to rise higher than those around them."

The salesman glanced toward the backseat at Nadya. "Don't you think so?"

Nadya only shrugged, but Ivan jumped in. "Absolutely!" he agreed with bombastic sarcasm. "Only the rich matter."

"You don't believe that," Sergei reminded Ivan.

"Life has opened my eyes," Ivan replied. "Humans are naturally greedy, selfish, and brutal. To expect anything more is to invite disillusion."

"Are you greedy, selfish, and brutal?" Nadya challenged him.

"Am I human?" he asked. "If so, then I am those things."

"Then you think I am also greedy, selfish, and brutal?" she said. "And Sergei too?"

"If pushed, you probably have those capacities," he insisted.

Sergei sighed to himself. It saddened him that his friend had become so cynical. When he'd first met Ivan, he'd told Sergei how he'd joined the Communist Bolsheviks in sympathy with their message of a decent life for all Russians, not only the aristocracy. He had been an idealist. But seeing the brutality of the Revolution had deeply wounded his spirit, and that wound had scarred over, leaving him with something hard and injured where his soul had been.

Lately Nadya had brought out something more playful in Ivan. Sergei had been glad to see it. So it made him especially disappointed to hear Ivan sounding so bitter now. It was almost as if he were trying to get back to acting like the cynical young man he had left behind these last few days. Maybe it made Ivan feel too vulnerable to laugh and be happy. Was he struggling to regain the untouchable heart he'd had before he met Nadya? Sergei wished—for Ivan's own happiness—that he wouldn't try so hard.

The salesman brought them into Moscow and even bought them supper, claiming that he couldn't stand to eat alone. Nadya fairly shoveled the meal into her mouth, making Sergei despair even further that he could ever teach her to be a grand duchess. They were all hungry, but the girl completely disregarded appearances. It made him wonder what the early years of her life had been like. Had no one ever taught her anything?

CHAPTER NINE
Changes

That night, Ivan brought them to the apartment of a soldier he had known while he was in the army. "He gave me the key," he showed them. The apartment was plain, but it had a bed, a couch, and an overstuffed armchair.

It also had a bathtub with a shower!

"You go first," Ivan told Nadya as he steered her to the bathroom. "Wash that filthy mop of yours."

"Don't tell me what to do!" she protested, shaking his hand from her arm. "It's not as though you smell like a flower."

"On second thought, come here and sit down," he insisted.

"Why?" she demanded.

"Just come. Come here." He took her arm and sat her down with an unceremonious push into a wooden chair.

Before Nadya could protest, Ivan had snapped up scissors that had been left on the table and chopped off the bottom of her hair up to her jawline.

Screaming, Nadya jumped up and stared at him, aghast. "My hair! How could you?"

"You'd never have gotten those knots out. And the short bob is the latest thing in Paris and New York. I saw it in a magazine," Ivan said, defending his action.

With tears in her eyes, Nadya raced into the bathroom, slamming the door behind her. Noisy sobs filled the apartment.

"That was a little brutal, don't you think?" Sergei criticized his friend.

"This is not a game!" Ivan said, his voice growing loud and agitated. "We have to find a way to make her presentable by the time we arrive in Paris, and we must do it by whatever means are necessary. Who would believe she was Anastasia with that awful hair?"

"A little kindness wouldn't kill you," Sergei argued.

Ivan stepped closer and lowered his voice. "That man she saw in the station," he began. "I think he was Secret Police."

"It's possible, I suppose," Sergei agreed. "Do you recall Rasputin's assistant?"

"I saw him once or twice during the Great War," Ivan said. "Sometimes he would stand on the balcony with Rasputin, beside the Imperial Family, during military parades and the like. What was his name?"

"I can't recall, but it occurred to me that he fit Nadya's description of the man at the station. Do you think he might have joined the Secret Police?" Sergei asked.

Ivan considered this. It certainly was possible. "Or he might still be working for agents of the Imperial Family, trying to track down Anastasia."

"True," Sergei agreed. "But perhaps he is a free agent working only for himself. The dowager empress is not the only one looking for Anastasia. Lenin has offered a reward for her return too. He doesn't want her leaving the country; she could be a powerful symbol for other Russians in exile to rally around. This new Communist government is not impervious to being overthrown. We will have to watch Nadya closely, for her safety."

"I've had the same thoughts," Ivan said as he crossed to the wardrobe and pulled out a large white shirt and a pair of his friend's trousers. "That's the other reason I cut her hair," he explained, laying out the clothing on the bed. "We'll all be safer if we disguise her as a boy."

"Safer from what?" Sergei questioned.

"From the Secret Police or anyone wanting to collect a reward from Lenin," Ivan said.

Sergei dropped his voice to a whisper. "By dressing her as a boy, do you think you're keeping yourself safe from your attraction to her?"

Ivan threw out his arm irritably, brushing off the remark. He might have grown to like this girl, but he was *not* attracted to her. He couldn't allow himself to be. It would ruin everything!

"Sergei, you really do say the stupidest things sometimes. Don't be an idiot!" he snapped.

CHAPTER TEN
In the Night Forest

As they traipsed from Moscow through the countryside of Russia, heading toward Germany on their way to France, Nadya was surprised to discover that she enjoyed life as a young man. It was freedom itself—no more hair to wash and tear a comb through; her clothing was loose and comfortable. Her walk was becoming bolder, with a hint of the swagger she'd so often observed in men; it was a way to ward off challenges to her "masculinity" from other young males who might be inclined to pick a fight with her.

The endurance and strength she'd developed during her year of hard, grueling work at The Happy Comrades served her well as they found itinerant day labor at ship docks, at cargo wharfs, or in fields, plowing the spring crops. They even found work swinging mallets to smash rocks in the employment of a builder of stone walls.

Nadya was strong enough to do the work alongside Ivan and Sergei, and every day she grew leaner and more muscular. It seemed to Nadya that they had, indeed, become "happy comrades." Working as equals to ensure their most essential needs—food, shelter, safety, and simple entertainment—had bonded them. Their shared goals and struggles had united the threesome in a way that she treasured.

Sergei, always so kind and upbeat, was like a brother to her, and even her initial up-and-down relationship with Ivan had now smoothed into one of friendship. Although they still spatted sometimes, it always was over quickly and their anger would swiftly abate. She could jolly Ivan out of a sour mood with a practical joke or a clever pun.

One evening, a month into their journey, as they made camp in the woods near the German border, Nadya bumped into Sergei while building their fire. He stared at her with surprise. "What is it?" she asked him.

"Your arms are rock solid," he remarked.

Proudly she rolled up the sleeve of her white shirt and flexed her biceps. "I love this life as a man," she told him honestly. "It's so free! I never want to go back to the confinement of being female."

She didn't like the distressed expression that came into his eyes. "Ivan!" he shouted.

Ivan had been collecting firewood in the forest but came running, tossing the wood he'd gathered as he blasted out of the trees. "What? What's happened?"

"Look at her arm!" Sergei demanded. "Flex it for him, Nadya."

With a grin, Nadya bent her arm, causing the muscle to bulge.

Ivan's eyes widened with exasperation. "You made me come running for that?"

"That is not the arm of a grand duchess," Sergei insisted. Taking Nadya's hand in his, he turned it palm up. "These calluses and those sunburned cheeks don't exactly make her look like a member of the aristocracy either."

"How do you propose that we live if she doesn't work?" Ivan challenged.

"I don't know, but we're on the German border; it won't be that long before we're in France. I've got to start training her to act aristocratically. As she is now, no one would even believe she'd even had a roof over her head, let alone lived in a palace. Nadya's looking more like a field hand than a grand duchess."

Ivan surveyed her, walking in a circle. "You're right," he agreed. "In many ways, she looks worse now than when we first found her."

"Precisely," Sergei said. "Back then she had a certain rough feminine appeal. She even had a natural delicacy. Now she looks like she was born to the hard work of the peasant class."

"Excuse me. I'm standing right here," Nadya irritably reminded them, "in case you forgot. I happen to like the way I look." These days, when she caught her image reflected in a lake while bathing or in the shining steel bumper of a harvester while working, she saw a young woman who stood tall with the health of days spent in the open air. There were no more dark circles under her eyes. The relentless sun had rid her complexion of its pasty pallor and had even splashed freckles across her cheeks. She did not miss the smoke-filled nights or the greasy food of The Happy Comrades Tavern. This hard but free life of honest labor was much better than the life of wasting away above the tavern, the life of scrambling hand-to-mouth on the street, or the life of squalid horrors she'd seen at the mental asylum. These were the happiest days she could recall.

"From now on, one of us will find work and get food while the other stays at the campsite and trains her," Sergei proposed.

"But I want to work," Nadya objected.

"You're right, that's what we will have to do," Ivan said to Sergei, ignoring Nadya's protest. "You train her in aristocratic manners and I will teach her how to be like Anastasia. We'll alternate days." He studied her once more. "No more haircuts," he declared.

"I like my hair short like this," she insisted.

"No. It's served its purpose. Now you've got to grow it long enough so you can style it."

"Since when did you become an authority on style?" she taunted. "Who do you think you are? Monsieur Ivan of Paris?"

She placed her hand on her hip and threw back her head in a mock imitation of Ivan as a stylist. "I will make you look divine. The time I have spent in the Russian Army has made me an expert on style. I will give you a Russian military cut—so chic! I call it the Red Army Bob."

"Very funny," Ivan replied dryly. "But listen to me. It's important. The Romanov sisters cared about fashion. The czar kept them in traditional, proper Russian attire, but Empress Marie sent the girls the latest style magazines from Europe. I found them all over the place at The House of Special Purpose."

"The House of Special Purpose": as Ivan spoke the words something went cold within Nadya. How ominous it sounded. When they named the place, they must have already known what its "special purpose" would be. Why else would they have called it that?

In the tavern, she'd heard men speak of the Romanovs with hatred, spitting out their names contemptuously, saying that they'd gotten no less than what they deserved for living so lavishly while the common people starved. Nadya also knew how it felt to have hunger gnaw at her insides like a raging animal. Hunger like that could turn a person savage with desperation. It was why she'd endured Mrs. Zolokov's abuse—because anything was better than starvation.

And yet . . .

When she saw photos of the Romanov family, she could not find it within herself to hate them. The little boy, Alexei, the czarevitch, was the youngest. He was rumored to have a sickness that would cause him to bleed to death if he were to get cut; he looked so sweet and fragile. The three oldest sisters were so elegantly beautiful in lacy white gowns with their blond hair swept up onto their regal heads, and the youngest one, Anastasia, was so playful and bright-eyed. All they'd ever known was privilege. How could they know their lives of luxury were an insult to those suffering in poverty?

"I don't want to be Anastasia Romanov!" Nadya blurted.

"What?" Ivan cried.

Unexpectedly, tears sprang to her eyes. "I don't want the life of a girl who could be extinguished at the whim of angry people, men and women she'd never even met, who don't know or love her."

Nadya sobbed and began to tremble. A warning sounded in the back of her mind—was this the madness, this passionate flame of wild emotion that had compelled her parents to dispose of her in the mental asylum? *Watch it*, the small voice of rationality warned inside her head. *Don't let it burn out of control or you'll scare off the only friends you have.*

It was no use! Nadya was being swept up by a wave of feeling that she felt helpless to harness. "What kind of people kill a girl who has done nothing but make up entertainments with funny characters or play harmless pranks on the servants? A girl who wanted nothing but to play catch with her little dog in the sunshine, but wound up watching everyone she ever loved murdered before she was also riddled with bullets?"

"How do you know these things?" Sergei asked.

"Because she was a girl and I was a girl. But why should I want *this* girl's life? Tell me!"

"It would be an easy life, a luxurious one," Ivan offered.

"Anastasia had the most lavish existence imaginable! And what did it get her? What?" Nadya shouted through her tears. "You tell me why I should do this; for what possible reason should I want this Anastasia's wretched life?"

Overcome with emotion, Nadya couldn't stand to look at them; Sergei gazed at her, incredulous at her outburst, while Ivan had his back turned as though disgusted.

Nadya was seized with an overpowering need to get away from them. With tears clouding her vision, she ran into the forest, pushing aside branches from her path as she went. With no thought to staying on a course or noting her direction, she ran until her foot slipped on a loose rock and flew up, launching her forward.

Nadya is in a voluminous, floor-length white nightgown, padding barefoot down a dark hallway. Her hand is outstretched against the wall for guidance as she heads toward a brilliant beam of light coming from the room at the end of this hall. She stops just short of the light and peers into an ornate, high-ceilinged room of murals and opulent furniture abundantly trimmed in gold.

The king and queen of Russia, Czar Nicholas and Czarina Alexandra, stand in the middle of the room. Nadya has seen their photos many times and recognizes them immediately. She realizes she must be in the Imperial Palace. How did she get in? Why is she in a nightgown?

The czar wears a white military-style jacket with golden braids and epaulets at the shoulders. He has on riding pants and boots, as though he might jump on a horse and ride off into battle at any moment. He has kind eyes. Alexandra is resplendent in a brocade cape lined with ermine fur, worn over a sparkling, full-length mauve gown.

The royal couple speaks to a large, hunched man in a filthy black cloak; he is a vile, ugly creature with a bulbous nose reddened from drinking and long, greasy black hair that clumps into sinewy tendrils. "I will not be dictated to!" he shouts, his tone threatening.

She knows who he is from newspaper photos—Grigory Rasputin! But Rasputin is dead.

All of them are dead. Is she seeing ghosts?

Then she reminds herself that she is in a dream. Anything can happen in a dream.

"We appreciate all you have done for our son, Father Grigory." Czar Nicholas speaks in a conciliatory way. "But I must insist that you keep a proper distance from the girls and their nursemaids from now on. Sura has complained that you come to do prayers with the girls when they are already in their nightgowns. They are not children anymore."

"Sura?" Rasputin questions.

"The girls' nurse," the czarina explains.

"Do you say this as well?" Father Grigory challenges her.

She cowers a little. "I know you are without blame," she says to soothe him, despite her obvious uneasiness, "but you visit the grand duchesses in their bedchambers when they are not dressed to receive company, and it causes talk."

"Let them talk! The name of Grigory Rasputin is known throughout Russia!" he bellows with rapturous grandiosity. "Everywhere, I am known as a holy man and mystic! You have seen my powers for yourself. I shall go back to St. Petersburg if I am not wanted."

"No!" the czarina cries. "You must not!"

"Ha!" he shouts triumphantly. "You know no other can stem the bleeding that ravages your boy, the future emperor."

"And for this, we are so very thankful," Czarina Alexandra assures him nervously.

"If I cannot visit the girls, how am I to tend to their immortal souls?" Rasputin challenges.

A man dressed in a black cape and black trousers approaches Grigory Rasputin. He is short but strongly built and has a twisting scar across his pale face.

That scar . . .

Nadya is suddenly in the Trans-Siberian train station. The man with the scar is chasing her.

It's a dream! It's a dream, she tells herself urgently.

But her terror is so real!

There is no one else in the station to help her. It's completely empty. The scarred man snatches at her, but each time she manages to duck away.

"I want the diamonds," the scarred man shouts, momentarily halting his pursuit. "They belong to me."

Nadya is still barefoot and in a white nightgown; her hair is no longer short but long and wavy. "Leave me alone. I don't know where they are. I don't!"

"I will have those diamonds," the man screeches, lunging at her.

She turns to run from him, and she hits a solid black wall. The stench of body odor tells her it is no inanimate obstacle. Looking up, she faces the sneering visage of Grigory Rasputin. Before Nadya can react, he seizes her shoulders in a crushing grip.

Nadya screams until the sound of her terror fills the station with a white noise so intense it becomes visible as a cloud of blinding illumination that obliterates everything.

"Nadya! Nadya!"

The all-encompassing white snapped into utter blackness.

Staring dazedly into the abyss of nothingness, Nadya began to see silvery forms gradually taking shape before her eyes; first the ovals of eyes appeared, then the slanting ridge of a nose. "Ivan?" Nadya asked the disembodied form hovering in the blackness above her.

"Thank goodness you're okay. I've been looking for you for hours. How'd you get down here? Are you hurt?"

"Where am I?" Nadya asked. Ivan's arm was around her now, and the solidity of and heat from his body was reassuring.

"You're at the bottom of some kind of ravine. I used my last match, or else I'd show you. You must have fallen and rolled down here. When I spotted you sprawled on the ground, I thought you were dead."

Shaken by this news, Nadya bowed her head and covered her face with her hands. "Oh God—I don't want to be dead."

Ivan tightened his hold around her. "No. No. Don't be dead. I'm so happy you're not dead." He kissed the top of her head. "Definitely don't be dead."

In the darkness, Nadya tilted back her head and reached up her hand until her fingers contacted the smooth surface of his lips.

Tenderly, he kissed her fingertips.

Then Ivan pulled her closer and sought out Nadya's lips with his own, kissing her gently at first, and then with growing passion. Nadya returned his kiss, somehow aware that all these days of traveling together had been leading them to this moment.

Ivan stroked Nadya's hair tenderly and then stood. Taking her hand, he drew her to her feet. "Do you feel well enough to walk?" he asked.

"I think so. Do you know the way back?"

Ivan hesitated uncertainly. "Not really," he admitted. "Let's see what we can find."

CHAPTER ELEVEN
Lessons in Royalty

By the time Nadya and Ivan finally had found their way back to the campsite, dawn's first rays were breaking. Sergei sat by the dying embers of their campfire. When he saw that they were back, he rushed to them. Thank goodness they'd returned. He'd been so worried!

Alarmed by the purple bruise on Nadya's forehead and the bump beneath it, Sergei reached out to touch her but then drew back, worried he might hurt her further. "What happened?" he asked.

"She fell," Ivan answered for her.

Nadya tapped the bruise and then cringed. "I had the most terrifying dream," she confided, and then, leaning against a boulder, went on to relay it to them.

Sergei looked to Ivan, his eyes full of questions. "She dreamed of Rasputin?"

"The whole country has nightmares about that charlatan," Ivan replied. "Did you know that Rasputin was not even his real name? It was a label given to him by the people of his village. It means something like 'dissolute' or 'disreputable.' Luckily, he's dead."

"From what I hear they had to poison him, shoot him, and then drown him before he would finally die," Sergei recalled.

"But he is gone?" Nadya was eager to confirm.

"That's what they say," Ivan told her. "We can only hope it's so. You know who he was, don't you?"

"I know what I've heard people say."

"But you've never met him?" Sergei pressed.

"How would I have?"

"You had a life before the asylum," he reminded her.

"A life at the Imperial Palace?" she questioned skeptically. "In my dream I was at the palace."

"I saw him once when I was a boy," Ivan said in a somber tone. "He was a bully and he smelled."

"When you drove the Imperial Family alongside your father?" Nadya said, remembering Ivan's story.

"You, then." I le stuck to his lie.

"The man from the train station was in my dream too," Nadya said.

Sergei looked at her sharply. "This man with the scar, you dreamed he was at the palace? You're sure it was him?"

"Yes, in the dream he was at the palace. I remember his hideous scar," she said. "It was probably just a crazy dream," Nadya decided. "The mind can concoct wild stories."

"Maybe not," Sergei said. Sergei was sure this was further confirmation that Rasputin's assistant and the man at the train station were the same. "Ivan, we should tell Nadya what we suspect about the man being Rasputin's assistant."

"We should," Ivan agreed. He told Nadya of their fears about the man. While they spoke together—Nadya full of questions that Ivan answered patiently and with reassurances that they would keep her safe—Sergei noticed that something between Nadya and Ivan had shifted. It was in the way they inclined toward each other ever so slightly, bending like plants toward the sun. There was a new softness in Ivan's eyes when he looked at her. Nadya's voice was gentler somehow.

If these were indications of new love, as Sergei suspected they were, then he was not surprised. All that scraping and arguing, the teasing and playful antagonism, could mean only one thing. It was a sure sign of attraction.

But now Sergei had a new worry. What would happen if this love blossomed? If everything went according to plan, what future could these two ever expect? None whatsoever; either their attraction to each other had to be stifled or their plan to pass off Nadya as the grand duchess Anastasia had to fail. Both events could not exist simultaneously.

That morning, Ivan went back to plowing fields for the farmer. How tenderly Nadya waved good-bye to him! It would have been touching if it were not so ill-fated.

Sergei and Nadya finished what they had left of yesterday's loaf of bread. Sergei went to a nearby stream to wash up, and when he returned he came upon Nadya seated on a blanket, her back to him. She was having a conversation with the small doll he'd noticed before. Unseen and unheard by her, he stood a way off and observed.

"So my little friend, what do you think?" Nadya asked the doll. "Will this turn out well?" She tilted her head, as if to hear the doll's reply. "You hope so? Well, that isn't very helpful! Will we regain our family? Will I find true love? Will everything be 'happily ever after' for us?" She did more pretend listening before continuing. "Oh, you're sure of it, you say? I'm so glad! No matter what happens, I know I can always talk to you, at least."

Sergei smiled gently, touched by how she loved this small remnant of her past. How many lonely nights it must have seen her through! Not wanting her to be embarrassed, he coughed loudly to announce his arrival.

Nadya turned sharply toward the sound and set the doll aside when she saw Sergei. "So, where shall we begin my training as a grand duchess?" Nadya asked brightly.

Sergei remembered how distressed she'd been the day before. "Are you feeling better about our endeavor?" he asked gently.

"If there's even a chance that I'm Anastasia, I should find out—and who would know better than the only living person who knew Anastasia, the Empress Marie? While we were trying to find our way back before, Ivan assured me that there would be no danger to Anastasia in Paris. That's what I felt most afraid of, that no matter where I went, I could never be safe if I were really the grand duchess."

"So now you feel willing to try?" he asked.

"Yes."

Sergei pondered their first lesson. The task was so vast that he was not sure where to begin. What was the first thing Anastasia might be called upon to do?

"Would you be able to write a letter introducing yourself to Empress Marie?" Sergei inquired. "A formal letter, I mean."

"I can write, if that's what you're asking," Nadya replied. "I don't remember how or when I learned, but I can do it."

"Very well," he said, fishing out a piece of folded paper—the unpaid hotel bill—from his pocket. He had brought along a nearly empty jar of ink and a fine-nib fountain pen—a remnant of his former privileged life—that he now took from the large pockets of his jacket. "Let's see how you do."

He presented the writing utensils and flattened the backside of the bill on an old plank of wood. "Pretend you're writing a letter to the empress," he suggested.

Nadya seated herself on a flat rock. With the

plank straddled on her knees, she thought for a moment before beginning. Sergei stood behind her, watching as she began to write: *Most beloved Grand-mother . . .*

"Why do you address her so?" Sergei asked.

"Isn't she my grandmother?"

"Why not Grandma or Dowager Empress Marie?"

Nadya tilted her head, perplexed. "I don't know. That's simply how it came to me."

"We must ask Ivan if he ever heard Anastasia address her grandmother," Sergei said, making a mental note to do so. If Ivan didn't know, then they would have to find out somehow. A wrong term of endearment would be just the sort of mistake to make the empress suspicious.

Sergei balanced on his haunches and peered over Nadya's shoulder to inspect her penmanship. It was the handwriting of one who had been schooled in the most excellent calligraphy. No one wrote in such a manner unless that person had been trained to do so. Every perfectly crafted letter curved uniformly, the *t* crossed with a confident slash, the capital G drawn in the grand old style. Her writing indicated education and wealth.

"You don't remember learning this at all?" he checked.

Nadya shook her head. "Everything before the asylum is a complete blank."

A fly hovered near the paper, smearing the ink.

Absently, Sergei brushed it aside, and then he jumped away as the last of the ink spilled across the paper.

Nadya jumped to avoid being splattered. "We can save that ink," she said, leaping toward her half-open pillowcase. Scooping up a ruffled white petticoat, she blotted at it. Twisting the fabric, she wrung precious drops back into the bottle. "Working with Mrs. Zolokov taught me to be a real cheapskate," she said with a smile.

"Ah, but now you've ruined your petticoat," he noted regretfully.

She tossed it aside, unconcerned. "It's an old thing; it barely even fits anymore. Apparently I was wearing it when Mrs. Zolokov found me. I don't think I've even put it on since that day. I should have left it behind, so at least it's served a purpose now."

Sergei lifted the worn white petticoat, curious to see if it could be salvaged; perhaps they could soak it in a pond and get the stain out. Examining the petticoat more closely, he saw brown stains that coincided with places where the fabric had been ripped through completely. Gunpowder stains? Could someone wearing this garment have been shot?

"Where did you get this?" he asked.

"Don't know," Nadya replied. "Maybe they gave it to me at the . . . you know . . . the asylum."

It was a gruesome possibility but was certainly plausible; an asylum might well refurbish clothing from the remains of the dead.

Sergei worked his fingers into the seams of the

waistband. The fabric seemed stretched, as though something had been in there before but had since been removed or had fallen out.

"Don't bother with that," Nadya insisted. "It doesn't matter. Let's get back to the letter. I saved enough ink, and I can squeeze out more from the fabric."

At the sound of pounding horse hooves, they both snapped their heads around toward the noise. Riders were bearing down upon them. With a protective instinct, Sergei stepped in front of Nadya to shield her from the two aggressively authoritative men emerging from the forest. "You are trespassing on the private estate of Count Dubinsky!" the first of the men stated with displeasure.

Sergei slowly grinned. "Count Yuri Grigorovitch Dubinsky?"

The burly man scowled with confusion. "The same," he confirmed.

"Then may I assume we have crossed the border into Germany?" Sergei asked.

The man nodded. "Indeed."

Sergei was pleased to discover they had traveled farther than he'd realized. He hadn't suspected it, as these men were speaking to them in Russian.

Clapping his hands with robust pleasure, Sergei stepped closer to the two horsemen. "We are not trespassers," he insisted. "We are friends come to visit Count Dubinsky."

The man pulled out a large firearm from under

his jacket. "Stand back!" he demanded. "Count Dubinsky does not fraternize with riffraff."

Sergei drew himself up to his full commanding height and squared his shoulders. "Tell Count Dubinsky that Count Sergei Mikhailovitch Kremnikov has arrived to see him."

CHAPTER TWELVE
Unexpected Developments

Ivan was standing in a half-plowed field under a threatening sky, examining a blister on his right hand, when a tidy, well-dressed man approached him. Ivan instantly assumed from the expression of authority on his face that the man was some sort of foreman bent on delivering a remonstrance to Ivan for pausing in his work. With that in mind, he snapped up the hoe he'd set on the ground and resumed work, despite the pain it caused his hand.

Ivan could not afford to be fired. As their sole support that day, he had a responsibility. If he were dismissed, there would be no supper for any of them tonight.

"Ivan Ivanovitch Navgorny?" the man inquired. When Ivan nodded, the man handed him an envelope.

Thoroughly baffled, Ivan opened it and found a card inside. It was a message in Sergei's writing. *We need you immediately. This man will lead the way. Go with him. Will explain when you arrive. Sergei.*

Ivan gazed at the messenger with troubled eyes. "Do you know what's wrong?" he asked.

The man spoke rapidly and seemed to be explaining that German was all he spoke. If Ivan hadn't been so worried, he would have been encouraged to discover they were so close to the border. His employer was Russian, so Ivan deduced that they were right on the line.

But what was this new trouble? Ivan knew they did not have the proper papers to cross the border. On foot, they were hoping to slip across the border undetected.

Somehow Ivan was sure this was the problem. Sergei and Nadya must have been picked up by the police as vagrants unable to produce the proper papers. It had to be.

Ivan gestured to the messenger, hoping to communicate that time was important. "Come, come on," he said. "Please take me to my friends."

The messenger understood and led the way across the field in the direction from which he'd come. Ivan wished the man would walk faster; he was anxious about his friends. If Nadya and Sergei were being sent back to Russia, he didn't want to get separated from them.

Of course, if Ivan were sent back to the Russian authorities, he risked arrest. This slowed his pace. He was a military deserter, after all. The penalty was to face a firing squad.

The German messenger noticed that Ivan had come to a near halt and looked at him questioningly.

Ivan felt pulled in two directions. If he stayed on the farm where he'd been working, he could avoid arrest. But Sergei had sent for him, and he was obliged by their bond of friendship to go.

But what if it were a trick? Perhaps Sergei had been forced to write the note. Maybe he was, at this very moment, hoping Ivan would see through it. The note was vague and cryptic, not at all like the loquacious Sergei. Could that be his friend's attempt to warn him that something was amiss?

And what of Nadya? Ivan knew he had gotten her into this. Wasn't it his duty to make sure she was all right?

Ivan's legs began moving again once he thought of Nadya. What was it he felt toward her? Friendship, certainly. When they'd first met he'd been sharp with her because he'd misjudged her. He'd assumed she was dim-witted and low-class because of where she worked and due to her messy appearance. When he'd heard about her being from an asylum, he'd been annoyed that he had taken on such a package of potential trouble.

And yet, there had been something he'd liked about her right from the start—even if it had taken him until now to admit it. Was it her spirit, her humor? Probably it was both.

Ivan had grown to respect not only her fun-loving attitude and intelligence, but also her resourcefulness, kindness, and tenderness. The only instability he could discern in her were the terrible nightmares that haunted her. And who was he to judge her for that, he who also knew what terrors sleep could bring?

Ivan had fallen in love with Nadya. There was no getting out of it, even though he knew not loving her would have been infinitely simpler. He loved her, like it or not. And really, down deep, he did like it so much. He loved the very sight of her, the sound of her voice, her laughter. He was inexplicably happy when she was near, and he had not felt happy about much for such a long time.

Propelled into a run by his thoughts of her, Ivan waved to the messenger to hurry. "Faster!" he cried. "I have no time to waste!"

The messenger caught up to Ivan and clapped him on the shoulder. He gestured toward an automobile parked on the dirt road bordering the farm, a Duesenberg roadster. Climbing behind the wheel, the man gestured for Ivan to join him.

The messenger led Ivan through ornately carved oak doors into the library of the palatial estate. Not since his childhood visits to the Peterhof Palace had Ivan been in a grander place. His mind raced as he sought to make sense of what was happening. Why was he here? It was not a government building. In Russia, the Bolsheviks had commandeered many of the wealthy's estates for their own use, converting them into housing for the poor masses or into government offices. But this estate still bore the earmarks of private ownership. Massive gold-framed oil paintings adorned the walls. Velvet drapes still festooned the impeccably clean, many-paned windows.

The moment Ivan stepped into the high-ceilinged room that boasted walls lined with leather-bound books, he was greeted by Sergei. "Ivan, at last!" his friend cried robustly. He was leaning with his arm propped on the mantel of a fireplace in which a roaring blaze crackled. "Please meet my friend Count Dubinsky."

A slight man with wispy blond hair sat in a high-backed leather armchair, and he now rose to greet Ivan. He wore a velvet lounging jacket over elegant black trousers. "Please consider everything at my house to be at your disposal," he said, gesturing around the room. "If it were not for the generous loan extended to me by Count Kremnikov, I never would have escaped the Revolution with my fortune intact."

Count Dubinsky's remark caused Sergei to roar with laughter. "Yes, I suppose you would be as penniless as we are right now," he remarked, "though for the life of me I can't picture you in anything other than finely tailored clothing and eating only the finest caviar."

"Well, until today that is the only way I could have imagined *you*," Count Dubinsky replied. "But have no fear. I have fared well in exile and am in a position to pay you back with interest."

"No, I could never charge interest," Sergei demurred.

"I insist. And I will pay you in German marks, which you will find vastly preferable to the now nearly worthless Russian ruble. You will discover that helping me out of the goodness of your heart was a wise investment. It doesn't come close to restoring the fortune you lost, of course. If only you had fled with me, as I'd wanted you to."

A cloud of unhappiness settled over Sergei's countenance, and Ivan was fairly sure he knew why.

"I couldn't leave until I'd received word that Elana and Peter had arrived safely in Sweden," he said. "I had to be available to aid them if they had encountered trouble, and then the Bolsheviks held me prisoner in my own estate for weeks."

"Why are you not in Sweden with them now?" Count Dubinsky asked.

"I do not know where they are," Sergei answered quietly. "They never arrived in Sweden."

"My good man!" Count Dubinsky cried with a gasp. "I am so sorry."

"Where is Nadya?" Ivan asked, eager to change the subject for Sergei's sake, as well as to be informed.

"Shopping!" Count Dubinsky told him enthusiastically, apparently pleased that they'd moved on to a less tragic subject. "My sister, Irina, has taken her to look at clothing and to have a day of beauty in the city. What a find you have made! It's almost unbelievable."

"I beg your pardon?" Ivan asked, looking to Sergei for an explanation.

"I confided in Dubinsky that we have tracked down the grand duchess Anastasia and intend to deliver her to her grandmother in Paris." A flickering sparkle in Sergei's eyes warned Ivan not to say anything that might indicate they were anything other than confident that Nadya was indeed Anastasia.

"Imagine the poor girl wandering the Ural Mountains all alone and without her memory until the good nuns took her in to their convent," Count Dubinsky said with emotion. "To think she might have lived out the rest of her days as a plain, humble nun."

"There are worse fates," Sergei remarked piously.

"Indeed," Count Dubinsky agreed with a somber air. "But she'd have lived without the knowledge of her birthright and her proper place in history."

Ivan was not surprised that Sergei had refrained from telling the count about Nadya's life in the asylum or her work as a tavern waitress. During the miles of walking, they had decided a convent was the most palatable and acceptable explanation of where Nadya had been since the Revolution. For their story they had concocted a fictitious convent they'd claim had been shut down by the Bolsheviks, who were well-known to be intolerant of religion.

"It's true she would have been robbed of her place in history. Very true," Ivan agreed. "Did you know the grand duchess before the Revolution, Count?"

"Quite so! I was a frequent visitor to the palace! As Sergei well knows, I had the ear of the czar himself. I was one of his most trusted advisers."

"And you have no doubt our Nadya is the same girl?" Ivan asked cautiously. Here was their first test. This man had seen the girl at her best, not just from afar or at the brink of death, as Ivan had seen her.

"None at all! Maturity has altered her, of course. Young people change so rapidly and radically during adolescence. I see no sign of her former aristocratic ways, but that's to be expected after spending time living as a hardworking nun."

"How do you think a grand duchess could have adapted to such plain living?" Ivan asked, thinking not of the convent but of Nadya's life on the streets and in the tavern.

"Strange as it may sound, she might have been oddly suited to such a life," Count Dubinsky said. "I will tell you something you might not have expected: Czar Nicholas insisted the girls live a somewhat spartan life. They slept on camp beds, and for many years he insisted they start each day with a bath made of ice water, just as he did. The czarina Alexandra, having been born in Germany and having spent many summers in England with her grandmother, Queen Victoria, was familiar with the luxurious life and often intervened on behalf of the girls. But mostly the czar held the line."

"Surely they lived in luxury, though," Ivan insisted, remembering the grand duchesses in their fine fur-lined coats, playing on their sleds or gliding over their private pond on glistening leather skates.

"It was an odd mix, to be sure. The czar was a doting father, but he didn't want his girls to grow up to be spoiled, either."

"Nadya . . . or I should start calling her Anastasia, I suppose. . . . She is very much a hard worker," Sergei observed.

"Oh, I'm sure she is. During the Great War the grand duchesses were frequently enlisted to stand in receiving lines, greeting and dispersing care packages for the soldiers for hours," Count Dubinsky recalled. "Of the four girls, Anastasia was the one who performed this duty with the most unflagging good cheer. If you have any doubt that your Nadya is she, let me show you a photo."

Count Dubinsky crossed the room and opened the top drawer of an elaborately carved desk. Sergei and Ivan joined him to see a photo of the count in the company of the czar and czarina, their four daughters, and their son, Alexei. Off to the right of the smiling group stood the scowling Father Grigory Rasputin.

Ivan's eyes immediately went to Anastasia, the youngest of the four girls all dressed in long, lacy white frocks. The three oldest had their hair swept up on the tops of their heads, but only Anastasia—probably because of her young age—kept her waves pulled up at the sides, gathered in a satin ribbon.

Ivan had been so right to select her! Those piercing, playful eyes burned into him from beneath straight brows. Nadya's eyes were the same. In the last month, hard work, outdoor living, and simple food had driven the gaunt, heavy circles from under them, and she looked even more like the grand duchess now than when he'd first met her.

"Of course the grand duchess would never be as sunburned and freckled as your Nadya," Count Dubinsky remarked. "The grand duchesses had the most flawless porcelain skin. The girls were always protected from the sun by a bonnet or a parasol."

"Well, now that I have run into you and we are once again funded, hopefully Anastasia's days of outdoor labor are over. She can regain her creamy complexion before we reach Paris," Sergei commented.

"She will not have as much time for this as you think, for I insist on putting my car and driver at your disposal. With a car, it's no more than a day's drive to Paris," Dubinsky said.

At this, Ivan and Sergei exchanged charged glances. Ivan knew they were thinking the same thing. This was a mixed blessing. A ride would be an incredible luxury, but it also advanced their timetable tremendously. They could, of course, linger in Paris until Nadya had been fully trained to act the part of Anastasia. On the other hand, time was of the essence. Who knew what impostors were approaching the empress Marie with girls trained to pose as her granddaughter? If the empress accepted one of them before Nadya arrived, it would be hard to change the woman's mind.

Suddenly, the doors to the library swung open and in strode the countess Irina Dubinsky. The count's short, dark-haired sister made a grand gesture of presentation, sweeping her arm wide. "Presenting the grand duchess of all the Russias, her Imperial Highness Anastasia Romanov."

Ivan turned to the open door. They all did.

No one appeared.

"Anastasia . . . Nadya?" Irina inquired as she headed back to the doorway to look for her. "Oh there you are," they heard her say as she disappeared into the hallway. Then there was some soft whispering before Irina drew Nadya reluctantly into the library, leading her by the wrist. "Doesn't she look gorgeous?" Irina asked.

Ivan gasped. "No! It's all wrong. I hate it!"

CHAPTER THIRTEEN
Controversy

Ivan's outburst prompted three separate reactions within Nadya. The first was to try to figure out what he disliked and promise to change it. Was it the permanent wave they'd had put in her hair; the new dress that billowed out around the bottoms of her calves; the newly plucked, now slightly arched eyebrows? Was the lipstick too red? She'd comb out her hair, burn the dress, fill in her eyebrows with pencil, and wipe away the lip color. She didn't want him to think she was shallow and silly.

But this lasted for only a moment. Nadya's second inclination to Ivan's unhappy, disapproving expression—and to her realization that it was in stark contrast to the smiles and admiration everyone else was showing—was to run from the room. To avoid the whole situation. The urge was strong, but she squelched it. Nadya realized this was something she did quite a bit, this running away when things became unpleasant. It was a habit she wanted to break. After all, she was not a child any longer and this new, more womanly look she'd put together with Irina's guidance made her feel even more powerful and more like an adult.

She chose to follow her third reaction: haughty defiance. Nadya recognized that this was often her fallback plan, but she didn't care. Unlike the running away, she wasn't sure this was a behavior she wanted to change. "Well, I like it," she said.

"You're crazy!" Irina Dubinsky ranted at Ivan. "She looks beautiful, like a princess or, I should say, like a grand duchess."

"She looks like a tart!" Ivan shot back.

Nadya stared at him, eyes wide and mouth agape. How dare he?

"The empress Marie will never think a girl dressed like . . . dressed like . . ." Ivan gestured at Nadya, his arm flailing as he struggled for the right word and failed to find it. "Like . . . *that*! She'll never think this is her royal granddaughter."

Wearing a disgusted expression, Irina waved him away. "Oh, you Russian men are all the same— old-fashioned prigs! You've been tied to the apron strings of stodgy Mother Russia for too long. You forget that the empress has been in Paris, the fashion capital of the world. She will know that this short hair with the Marcel Wave is the latest thing."

"You even mentioned the hair before," Sergei reminded Ivan.

"This dress is a Parisian designer original," Irina continued, signaling for Nadya to turn and give the dress a spin. "The high-heeled shoe with an ankle strap is being shown in all the magazines. She has the look of a modern woman."

"She is an aristocrat, not a flapper!" Ivan cried.

"Where did you learn that term?" Sergei asked.

"I can read magazines too, you know!" Ivan replied.

"You'll get used to it," Count Dubinsky told Ivan with a jovial air of conciliation. "You simply need to adjust to the change. You're not in Russia anymore."

Nadya pleadingly met Ivan's eyes. For the first time that she could remember, she felt pretty. She wanted him to think she looked attractive.

Sergei stepped forward and circled her. "What happened to the bruise on your forehead?" he asked Nadya.

"Makeup," Irina answered.

Sergei turned to Ivan. "I say she looks very pretty," he decided. "You have to admit that, Ivan."

Ivan's expression softened, and his body seemed to melt toward Nadya. "You do look lovely, Nadya . . . really pretty."

Her heart soared. She knew she must be beaming like a child, grinning like some simpleminded fool, but Nadya was helpless to stop.

"I'm just not convinced it's the right look to win over the empress," Ivan added.

Irina came alongside Nadya and wrapped her

arm protectively around her waist. "Well, we bought many outfits. You may find some of them more to your liking than this dress—though I happen to think it is *très chic.*"

"I don't have to wear so much makeup," Nadya offered as a compromise.

Irina scowled at her. "Don't let him bully you. You look fabulous just as you are."

"You do," Sergei agreed.

"Now whose side are you on?" Ivan chided him.

"I'm not on any side. The girl looks beautiful this way. Only an old stick-in-the-mud would think otherwise," Sergei replied.

"I just said she looked pretty, didn't I?" Ivan testily defended himself. "The look is just not appropriate."

"I have an idea," Count Dubinsky said. "Why don't I throw a big party for you? There are a great number of White Russian exiles living in the area. We will introduce the once lost and now rediscovered Grand Duchess Anastasia, and we'll see how they accept her. It will be a sort of trial for meeting the grand empress."

"But there's still so much I have to fill her in about," Sergei objected. "She doesn't remember anything about life at the palace."

"Nor should she," Count Dubinsky said. "She has been traumatized and has suffered amnesia."

"But wouldn't she have retained her aristocratic bearing even if her memory was lost?" Ivan questioned.

"Though Anastasia was a very natural girl even in her most splendid finery, she had an inherent elegance," Count Dubinsky said, studying Nadya as he spoke. "I see that innate grace in Nadya. I don't think there's much work left to be done."

Nadya felt an urge to wrap up the skinny little count in a hug and kiss his cheek. In the last month she'd felt like she was being groomed and schooled for some big exhibition. The count now was saying she was fine as she was, and Nadya was grateful for his encouraging words.

"What do you say to that proposal?" the count asked them.

Everyone excitedly spoke at once, all saying it was a wonderful idea. But Ivan shouted above the others in disagreement. "*She's not ready!*"

They all quieted and gazed at him. "She must be ready," Sergei said in a matter-of-fact tone. "There's no time left. She simply has to be ready."

"Ready? What's to be ready?" Irina cried, throwing up her hands in exasperation. "She's beautiful. She's young. What more do you need? They'll adore her!"

"But will they think she's Anastasia?" Ivan pressed.

Irina held him in a steely, meaningful gaze. "Do you think she's Anastasia?"

"I do . . . yes . . . of course," Ivan stammered.

Irina reeled on Nadya. "Do *you* think so?"

Nadya could feel herself coloring with embarrassment. "I'm . . . I'm not sure," she admitted.

"Naturally she's not sure," Sergei blustered. "She's been through so much. Her memory is gone. It's perfectly normal that she would have blocked out so much of . . . of everything."

Irina looked from Sergei to Ivan to Nadya and thoughtfully rubbed her chin with narrowed, suspicious eyes. Crossing to Nadya, she took ahold of her wrist. "Come with me," she said, leading Nadya out of the library. "It's time for a woman-to-woman chat."

CHAPTER FOURTEEN
Struggles

"Why are you so agitated?" Sergei demanded of Ivan once Nadya and Irina were gone. Count Dubinsky also had gone to consult with his chef about lunch, and the two were alone in the library.

"Are we really going to present her to the world as Anastasia at this party?" Ivan asked. "Don't you think that's dangerous? There will be Russian émigrés who knew the Imperial Family."

"But Dubinsky is right. Don't you see?" Sergei said. "We simply say she lost her memory. And it is true!" The moment the count had suggested it, Sergei had wondered why they hadn't thought of it themselves. Here they were, about to embark on the arduous, nearly impossible task of training a common-born girl to behave like royalty when all they had to do was claim she had amnesia. Since Nadya really *did* have amnesia, the plan should have been obvious to them from the start.

"It won't work," Ivan insisted. "Even if Anastasia had lost her memory, she wouldn't be as rough as Nadya."

"I don't find her to be all that rough," Sergei disagreed. In fact, the more he got to know Nadya, the more he saw a natural refinement in her. "She has the most exquisite handwriting," he recalled.

"But she doesn't know royal things," Ivan objected.

"*Amnesia*," Sergei reminded him.

Ivan disgustedly waved him away as he turned. "What if she doesn't fit in with this bunch of aristocrats Dubinsky is inviting, and they make her feel foolish? She might lose her confidence and refuse to go the rest of the way to meet the empress. Then all our efforts will have been for nothing. We'll have wasted all this time, and we won't get the reward money!"

Sergei watched his friend for a moment without speaking. What a complex fellow he was! Why did he insist on cloaking his decent, even sensitive, nature with a facade of put-on callousness? Sergei was almost certain Ivan had fallen in love with the girl, but here he was insisting, yet again, that all he cared about was the reward money.

"We'll spoil everything if we rush her," Ivan muttered.

"Are you afraid she won't pass the test or are you trying to shield her from embarrassment?" Sergei probed. He suspected that Ivan was protecting Nadya—another possible way that this brewing romance was complicating things.

"Maybe a little of both," he admitted, still staring into the fire.

"I thought so." Sergei settled onto the leather couch. "Believe me, my friend, I feel just as protective of Nadya. I've had my second thoughts about all this, as you well know. One thing worried me in particular," he said.

"What is that?" Ivan asked.

"By presenting Nadya to the empress, aren't we stopping her from finding her real family? Maybe somewhere her true family is looking for her." As Sergei spoke these words, a lump formed unexpectedly in his throat. What if somewhere his wife Elana still lived and was down on her luck, struggling to support their son on her own? Sergei imagined a scenario where she agreed to pose as Anastasia for two con men like themselves. If Elana succeeded, she might pay someone to raise Peter while she lived out the rest of her days posing as someone she was not. If Elana were to live life as Anastasia, he might never find her at all. "Maybe what we're doing isn't right," Sergei suggested. "We're not being honest with the empress or fair to Nadya or her family, if she has one."

"You've picked a fine time to worry about all this!" Ivan exploded.

"Perhaps, but I had to mention it."

"Sergei, you're a dreamer! Anastasia is dead. Empress Marie is never going to find her because she is not alive. Nadya's family has abandoned her. If they ever were looking for her, she wasn't that difficult to find, working right there in a tavern in the middle of Yekaterinburg. And just because you're about to be repaid a borrowed sum of money doesn't mean your fortune has been restored to you. We still need that reward money; otherwise we have nothing!"

"But is it right?" Sergei asked, anguished.

"It's right to unite the empress with her granddaughter. The empress is a lonely old woman, and she wants Anastasia back. Nadya was a girl living alone in squalor. She might have married some miner who wandered into the tavern, but now she'll marry a prince, or a duke, or maybe a wealthy American captain of industry."

"And you wouldn't mind that?" Sergei questioned.

Ivan swung around to face him, apparently surprised by the question. "Me? Mind? Why would I mind?"

Sergei cast Ivan an impatient look. "Nothing happened the other night in the forest? There was no kiss?" Sergei pressed.

"No."

He didn't believe it. Something had happened. He could see it in both their faces. "You're lying."

"I'm not," Ivan insisted.

"Why do you pretend to be so cold all the time?" Sergei cried, jumping impatiently to his feet. "It's all right to have feelings!"

"No it's not!" Ivan shouted back. "Not for me. I

was friends with the soldiers I fought beside. I loved my country so much I lied about my age to enlist. I was battling Germans on the Eastern Front when I was only fifteen, and I saw my friends die in droves. I believed in Communism as the great hope of Russia until I saw the cold-blooded nature of my fellow Communists. No, sir! This life has knocked the ability to feel right out of me."

"And to think that this morning I was sure you were happy," Sergei said sadly.

"Maybe for a moment. But then I came here and remembered I would be giving Nadya up to the empress in a few days. I can't afford to feel anything for her."

"That's what I've been trying to tell you, you fool," Sergei said emphatically. "What if we *don't* bring her to the empress?"

"We have to!"

"Why?"

"Because it's the right thing for Nadya," Ivan said with resigned sadness. "You saw that photo Dubinsky showed us. She looks just like Anastasia. The empress is bound to accept her. What other chance does she have to live a life like that? If I hold onto her for my own selfish reasons, she will never have an opportunity like this again."

Sergei sat again, folding his arms, certain that all his suspicions had been confirmed. "I see," he said. "I don't know if I've ever heard a truer declaration of love."

CHAPTER FIFTEEN
An Explosion of Diamonds

Irina shut the door to her spacious bedroom. It was an elegant room with a canopied bed that matched the fabric of her smooth, glossy damask curtains. Irina indicated that Nadya should be seated on the cushioned chair at her vanity desk. "So, do you love him too?" she asked abruptly.

"Who?" Nadya asked cautiously.

"Ivan, of course! It's clear enough that he's in love with you."

Nadya felt something light and fizzy rising from within her. She hadn't ever felt this way before—she was almost giddy with the sensation. "Do you really think . . . I mean . . . Ivan is in love with me?"

"Oh, please. Don't be thickheaded! What man who isn't head over heels would be that overprotective and jealous?"

"Jealous of what? Of whom?"

"Of all the attention you'll be getting when everyone sees what a beauty you are."

"Me? No." Nadya was not being modest or fishing for further compliments; she simply did not see herself as a beauty. Yes, she felt prettier than ever before, but beautiful?

"You are very beautiful, just like your mother and sisters. You've grown to look a great deal like them, in fact, though the last time anyone saw you, you were only on the brink of young womanhood."

"Did you and I know each other?" Nadya asked.

"No. My brother liked life at the palace, but I preferred our country manor. I've seen pictures, though. Do you honestly remember nothing?"

"Nothing."

"That may be just as well considering what . . . what happened." Irina sat on the edge of her bed and gazed at Nadya with sympathy. Reaching forward, she took her hand. "Thank God the nuns took you in."

"I wasn't in a convent," Nadya confided, feeling she could trust Irina. "First I was in an asylum, then I lived on the street until I found work at a tavern. Ivan and Sergei thought it would be best not to tell the sordid details of my real life." She went on to tell her about everything she could recall of her time in Yekaterinburg.

As she listened, Irina blanched noticeably. "How awful."

"I don't understand how I landed in the asylum," Nadya said. "Do I seem deranged to you?" To lighten the moment, Nadya crossed her eyes and comically twisted her face.

Irina laughed. "Stop that, please! No, I didn't think you were unbalanced at all, at least not until now."

"Well see, there you are!" Nadya said, smiling despite the seriousness of the subject. "Maybe I'm *not* right in the head."

"Anastasia always was known for her joking. Your making light of this only further assures me that you are she."

"I'm not so sure," Nadya admitted. "Though I do have the most frightening dreams."

"It makes sense, in a way, that you might be hidden in an asylum," Irina allowed. "There you were, a young woman wandering around with no idea of your identity. Committing you would probably be the best way for the local police to ensure your safety."

"That makes sense," Nadya allowed. "So you really believe I'm Anastasia?"

"Yes. Don't you?" Irina asked.

"Sergei and Ivan are convinced, and I trust them," Nadya said. "Other than that, I have no way of knowing. Sometimes Grigory Rasputin appears in my nightmares, but so do dragons, gargoyles, and other monsters. I once dreamed I was being chased by Lenin, and I'm pretty sure, from what I've heard, that he never knew Anastasia."

"I agree that dreams are not reliable." Irina patted Nadya's hand and smiled as if to put the conversation to rest. "If my brother is sure you are the grand duchess, then I am sure. Now you still haven't answered my question: Do you love Ivan?" Irina pressed.

"We've kissed," Nadya admitted. "Just last night for the first time."

"So I was right. But do you love him?"

"He can be very annoying," Nadya considered. "He's also stubborn and sometimes full of himself."

"I noticed," Irina remarked. "But he's very good-looking, and he becomes tender when he's near you."

"Do you think so?" Nadya asked hopefully. There was that light frothy fizz rising inside of her again.

"Absolutely. What's his title?"

"Title?"

"Sergei is a count. My brother is a count. I am a countess. You are a grand duchess. What's Ivan's title?"

The idea of this made Nadya laugh. She couldn't imagine Ivan with a title. "He has none."

"You mean he's just . . . a . . . commoner?" Irina said, clearly aghast.

"His father drove the coach for the Imperial Family, and he used to accompany him. That's how he knew Anastasia and why he's so sure of my identity."

"He's the son of a coach driver?"

"I don't see anything wrong with that."

Irina rose and headed toward the door. Her brow was furrowed in thought. "You look tired, Nadya," she said. "Why don't you have a nap before lunch?"

"That sounds good," Nadya said, stretching. "Irina?"

"Yes?"

"You seem worried. What are you thinking?"

"You never said you loved Ivan, and I'm thinking that—in light of what you've just told me—it's probably best that you don't."

It took a moment for Nadya to fully register the meaning of Irina's comment. She should not love Ivan because he wasn't *royal*? That struck her as so terribly wrong!

Nadya opened her mouth to argue but, instead of speaking, her nostrils flared as she suppressed a yawn. She was tired and her head was beginning to throb. She desperately needed to sleep. She would think about everything when she awoke.

"I will see you in a little while, after you nap," Irina said as she left.

Snuggling under the bed covers in the middle of the day made Nadya feel divinely decadent. It was lovely, like drifting to sleep in the soft petal center of a rose. Somewhere in her buried past there had been a similar room. Where?

As she worked to resurrect this forgotten memory, Nadya succumbed to the luxurious softness of the bed, letting it lull her to sleep.

Nadya is in another sleeping quarters, which is aglow in amber light. Four plain cots stand side by side in a row. The room is empty. Because it is a dream, she cannot tell where she is in the room. Maybe she is in a wardrobe, watching. Perhaps she is outside, looking into the room through a keyhole.

The sinister figure of Grigory Rasputin sweeps in and begins to pace with restless impatience. Nadya chafes with the powerful urge to spring from her concealment and chase him away, shouting with arms flailing, but she doesn't dare. He is too terrifying. He emanates dark menace, almost pulling the light from the room.

After more interminable pacing from Rasputin, the queen, Czarina Alexandra, enters. She shuts the door behind her. "This is not a good place to meet," she whispers, clearly upset. "You're not supposed to be in the girls' quarters. Why are we meeting here?"

"Because it's mealtime, and I knew we would be alone. You had no trouble getting away?"

"I said I had a headache."

"Well?" Rasputin asks irritably. He expectantly presents a gnarled hand with yellowed nails, palm out. "Where is it?"

Alexandra draws a satin bag from the voluminous pleated sleeve of her gown. From it she takes out the most spectacular diamond necklace Nadya has ever seen. It hardly looks real! Three strands of outsize diamonds, each increasing in size as they approach the center, culminate in a rectangular-cut blue diamond of such brilliance that it appears to shine from within.

The czarina places the sparkling gem necklace into Rasputin's waiting hand. "This was my mother's," she says sadly. "It once belonged to Marie Antoinette."

Nadya expects Rasputin to be in awe of his prize, but

he seems oddly unimpressed. "A small price to pay to preserve the life of the future czar of All the Russias," he says in a mocking tone.

Then Count Dubinsky rushes in with a tall, thin, princely personage dressed regally under a cape. "Prince Yuperov and I have come to stop you from making this terrible mistake," Count Dubinsky tells Alexandra. "We had heard rumors that he was demanding enormous payment for helping poor Alexei with his illness. We have been watching him closely for days, and now we have caught him at it."

Rasputin possessively clutches the necklace to his chest.

"This necklace is mine to give as I choose," Alexandra insists.

"The czar may not agree," says Prince Yuperov. "It became part of the Imperial Estate when you were married. If news gets out that you have given the necklace to this charlatan, the people will be outraged. There is much discontent as it is over the amount of Russian wealth being bestowed upon this fraud."

The next thing Nadya knows, there is a scuffle as Prince Yuperov struggles to take the necklace from Rasputin. The necklace flies into the air, and then it shatters in an explosion of sparkling light as the jewels hit the floor.

Rasputin, Prince Yuperov, Count Dubinksy, and even the czarina scramble to snap up the broken strands of glittering diamonds. "We will go to the czar and tell him about this!" announces Prince Yuperov, dashing from the room clutching a portion of the necklace. Everyone rushes out behind him.

Nadya is alone again. From under the last cot, something shimmers like a fallen firefly, and she dares to leave the cover of her hiding place to approach it.

Lying on her stomach, she slides under the cot and scoops out a single diamond that has come loose from its setting. The adults seem to have recovered all the other diamonds but this one.

This misplaced yellow-tinged gem does not possess the showy grandeur of the center blue diamond, but it is spectacular nonetheless, surely one of the larger stones from near the middle of the necklace.

Suddenly a man steps in front of Nadya. It is the scarred man from the train station.

Terrified, Nadya screams.

Nadya awoke screaming. Quieting as she realized it had been a dream, she clutched her head in anguish. Would these awful nightmares ever stop?

CHAPTER SIXTEEN
Anastasia Is Presented

Two nights later, Ivan studied his tuxedo-clad image in the full-length mirror. He had to admit that he looked good. This was the first time he'd ever worn such an outfit.

Downstairs, the quartet the count had hired for the party was warming up. Punching his fist into his open palm, Ivan began to pace anxiously. Either these aristocrats would accept Nadya as Anastasia or all three of them would be condemned as frauds. They'd convinced Dubinsky and his sister easily enough, but this would be the real test.

Sitting on the edge of his bed, Ivan pictured how the evening might play out. Nadya would be overwhelmed and confused about how to behave with the aristocrats. She wouldn't know what fork to use for her salad or would fail to understand all their references to the sophisticated worlds of classical music and fine art. The guests would begin to look at Nadya askance and would speculate among themselves. They might think the girl was too common and uneducated to be the lost grand duchess.

Ivan pictured Nadya upset. He saw himself consoling her, telling her not to worry. At least they had found each other. They would return to Moscow together, never again to be parted.

Ivan stood abruptly and shook his head. "No!" It was not acceptable to wish for failure. He had set out to make a large sum of money and to change his life. He would take his half of the reward but would not return to Russia at all. He'd stay in Paris and begin life anew, without the threat of being arrested for deserting the army. Nothing could deter him from that, certainly not anything as whimsical and fleeting as an infatuation with a tavern girl.

And a tavern girl was exactly what she was; there was no point in convincing himself that she was anything other than that. If Ivan was being brutally honest, though, he had to admit that he had started to confuse Nadya with the girl he'd seen there in the woods.

Unbidden, a picture from that day returned to him. He saw the slim, sun-dappled figure in her gauzy dress as she had stood seconds before she fell. In slow motion, he remembered how Anastasia's arm had reached into the air, how gracefully her back had arched as she danced that hideous ballet with death.

Ivan remembered then what he had never before allowed himself to recall: a split second when they had locked eyes. She had looked to him as if asking for advice: *What should I do?*

Ivan could not have helped. Aghast with horror, he had no plan of escape to offer her. But they had shared this terrible moment together—and in that split second, he had given his heart to her.

In that moment just before she'd died, Ivan had fallen in love with the grand duchess Anastasia Romanov. His was the last face she had seen. Hers was the face he would see over and over in his dreams forever more.

Sergei knocked on the door and stepped inside. In his tuxedo, he looked every inch the aristocratic count he'd once been. "Ready?" he asked cheerily.

"Aren't you the least bit nervous?" Ivan asked.

"No. She'll do just fine. People will understand that she's lost her memory."

"But do people with amnesia lose all memory? Do they forget what they've learned of art and culture?" Ivan asked desperately.

"I don't know," Sergei admitted. "I've never personally known anyone else with amnesia. But I'll tell you one thing she hasn't forgotten: She writes in the most exquisite script."

"Are you saying there's some breeding and culture in her background?"

"I don't know how else she'd write like that."

"Well, let's hope she draws on that mysterious

background of culture tonight," Ivan said. "She'll need every bit of it."

They went downstairs together, as Count Dubinsky's guests were starting to arrive. Sergei knew many of them from the days when they'd traveled in the same aristocratic circles in Moscow. Ivan stood at Sergei's side, smiling blandly and shaking hands as he was introduced to the various counts, countesses, dukes, duchesses, barons, baronesses, and even princes and princesses. It hurt Ivan to see the pain in his friend's eyes whenever someone inquired after his wife and son. Each time Sergei said the same thing: "We became separated while fleeing the Bolsheviks. If you hear anything of them, please send word to Count Dubinsky."

There were close to a hundred guests assembled in the grand ballroom, eating small pancakes topped with caviar and sipping flutes of champagne, when a servant opened the painted doors on the far side of the room.

Irina stepped into the grand room, dressed in a black gown with a purple lace shawl, and addressed the crowd. "Thank you for joining my brother and me on this very special evening. Tonight, as promised, we wish to present you with a most wonderful surprise. It is our delight to present to you our guest of honor, a most beloved personage whom we had all despaired we would not see again. It is with the deepest joy that I present to you Her Imperial Highness, the grand duchess Anastasia Nicholaevna Romanov!"

An astonished gasp swept through the crowd of guests.

Ivan drew in a deep breath and held it.

Wearing an expression of utter panic, Nadya stepped into the doorway. She wore a shimmering strapless blue gown that skimmed her form like water as it flowed to her feet. Elbow-high white gloves accompanied the dress, and Ivan silently thanked Irina for her thoroughness in assembling the outfit. He never would have thought of gloves, and he doubted that Nadya would have, either, but it wouldn't have done to have her shaking hands with those work-worn, calloused palms.

Nadya's short blond hair was swept up in a slim blue headband and topped with elegantly small curls that Ivan knew had to be a hairpiece but looked lovely nonetheless. If they'd consulted him, Ivan would have vetoed makeup. But he had to admit, the light blush of rouge on Nadya's cheekbones highlighted them to dramatic effect, and he'd never realized her eyes were as startlingly blue as they appeared now, ringed with liner and mascara.

A moment of awed silence passed as everyone stared at Nadya, the phantasm returned from the grave. The silence was broken when a heavyset countess cried out passionately, "*Das Vedanta!* Hail to Mother Russia!"

The crowd took up the cry as they swarmed forth to embrace their lost princess, the living symbol of all that once had been. Many women and even some men wept openly and without shame. "Give her room. Let her breathe," Irina firmly cautioned, guiding Nadya through the affectionate, murmuring crowd.

Sergei chuckled with triumphant glee. "What do you think of our girl now, eh?"

Ivan didn't answer. His thoughts were on the image of a man he'd detected skulking outside a window. The man had peered in, riveted by the sight of Nadya as she had stood in the doorway, so much so that he'd stepped into sight, forgetting to hang back in hiding. Quickly, though, he'd recovered his wits and had darted back away from the window, but not before Ivan had gotten a look at him. He was a short, dark-haired man with a ragged, twisted scar curling across his face.

CHAPTER SEVENTEEN
The Face at the Window

Sergei watched from the party sidelines as Ivan leaped to the window, peering out frantically, as though searching the night for some threat. Setting down his untouched flute of champagne, Sergei hurried to join his friend at the window. "What is it?"

"The man Nadya saw at the station—I think he's out there," Ivan reported.

"Impossible!" Sergei asserted, but Ivan already was off toward the front door. Sergei instinctively followed. "Do you see anyone?" he asked, joining Ivan on the wide outdoor steps.

Jumping athletically to the bottom, Ivan swatted the adjacent bushes in an effort to drive out the intruder, but it was to no avail. "I swear he was there, Sergei. He had the most awful scar, just as Nadya had described him."

Sergei scanned the grounds, but all that moved

were the rustling leaves stirred by the evening breeze. "Do you think it was the same man from the station?" he asked Ivan.

"It could be," Ivan replied.

"He must be after Nadya. He missed his chance to get her at the train station, and now he's biding his time since he's out of his jurisdiction," Sergei suggested. "Let's get back to the party. We've left her alone inside."

Together they raced back into the ballroom. Anxiously, Sergei scanned the crowd for Nadya and, with a sigh of relief, found her encircled by a group of fawning guests, chatting amiably.

Sergei could hear her bright, contagious laughter through the crowd, and it made him smile. He had come to know its sound so well. How radiant she was tonight! "She is every bit a grand duchess," Sergei said to Ivan.

Ivan didn't seem to hear him as he stared at Nadya with rapt attention. It was as though Ivan was spellbound.

A young man in tails crossed the room, bringing her a plate of food. Another approached from a different direction with a flute of champagne. Nadya smiled graciously at both of them before setting both the food and the drink on a nearby table. The two men didn't even notice that Nadya had set aside their gifts, she'd done it with such deft grace, smiling at them all the while.

The quartet struck up a waltz. Sergei watched as

Ivan slid through the circle of admirers surrounding the radiant Nadya. With a quick but gallant bow, he invited her to dance. She smiled and accepted.

Ivan whirled Nadya out onto the dance floor, creating a buzz of excitement. He swept her along in time with the music, and the two melted together in an effortless flow of movement. How good they looked—he so handsome and confident, she the very image of grace and beauty!

The way Nadya leaned into Ivan's arms moved Sergei to think of other dances long ago when he'd held his Elana in much the same way. The two of them had been deeply in love, and so when he saw Ivan and Nadya together, Sergei recognized the body language.

With a pang of nerves, Sergei scanned the party's sidelines in search of this mysterious scarred man. He saw no one who fit the description—nor anyone who looked like Rasputin's assistant—and he gradually began to relax a little. The man had probably run off, realizing that Ivan had caught sight of him.

Sergei seated himself on a velvet chair to consider their situation. What a success Nadya had made of this evening! After tonight, word would spread like a rampant wildfire that a member of the Romanov Imperial Family had miraculously survived.

White Russians loyal to the Romanovs were scattered all over Scandinavia, Europe, and even Asia. Before this party even was over, word would most likely reach some of them via telegrams. By the morning, talk of counterrevolution—of reclaiming Imperial Russia with the czarina Anastasia on the throne—would probably be swirling. The excitement would be widespread. It was likely that the empress Marie would already be expecting them by the time they arrived in Paris.

For the most part, this was all good. The more the world embraced Nadya as Anastasia, the more at ease she would become. This general acceptance would encourage the empress to see Nadya as her granddaughter as well.

The immensity of what Ivan and he were doing impressed itself on Sergei for the first time, and he drew in a deep breath to calm himself. How had he not seen it before? Was he a fool? How had he not realized they were about to unleash a political whirlwind with tremendous consequences in Russia, possibly even the world?

They hadn't intended to start a counterrevolution!

It hadn't even occurred to them. But tonight, seeing the light of excited fervor that the sight of Anastasia had rekindled in the eyes of these exiled Russians, he knew they'd gotten themselves into something much bigger than they'd expected.

The sudden notoriety that would surely follow made the man with the scarred face even more dangerous. It would be all the more difficult to slip past him now.

Just how dangerous was he?

Out on the dance floor, Ivan had his left hand

planted on Nadya's waist as he expertly steered her around the dance floor. He'd mentioned to Sergei that one of the many odd jobs he'd worked was as a ballroom dancing instructor's assistant. It showed. But Nadya—where had she learned to dance with such fluid ease?

Nadya *must* have been brought up and educated in a wealthy family. But then why had no one come looking for her when she went missing? Maybe her family was dead; the Bolsheviks had been merciless to the aristocracy and the upper classes.

The poor girl; she'd been through so much. It was good to see her so radiantly happy, as she appeared to be, there on the dance floor in Ivan's arms.

Were they bringing her to a happy life or ushering her into a strange world of political intrigue? Or—and this sent a chill down Sergei's spine—by having her pose as Anastasia were they as good as signing her death sentence?

The music stopped. Though the other dancers left the dance floor, Ivan held Nadya in his embrace. Her head rested on his shoulder as they swayed together to a love song only they could hear.

Chapter Eighteen
Summoned to Paris

The next morning Nadya lay in bed, still not asleep despite the fact that the first gray light of dawn had begun to seep through the curtained windows, lifting her bedroom from darkness. She'd lain there sleeplessly for no more than three hours. The party had lasted far into the night, and then they'd stayed up another hour more, sitting by the fire and gleefully rehashing the triumphant evening.

What a night it had been! Life as Anastasia was so glamorous! The guests had plied her with eager questions all night. When they had asked if she recalled them from her palace days she'd simply apologized for her amnesia. Others had wanted to know about her life in exile. In this instance she'd simply concocted stories about her time with the nuns. It all had come so naturally to her. Not a single skeptical eyebrow had been raised.

When Nadya had sat down to dinner and had to make sense of the wide assortment of dining utensils, she'd simply employed her common sense or had watched the other guests. It had worked too! Using the outside utensils and working inward with each new course turned out to be exactly the correct approach.

Toward the end of the evening, Irina had linked her arm into Nadya's and had whispered in her ear, "Guests who have met Anastasia are saying they have no doubt you are the grand duchess."

Now Irina's words kept replaying in her mind. *They had no doubt!* These guests had known Anastasia and they were convinced that she, Nadya, was the youngest daughter of Nicholas Romanov, Czar of All the Russias.

So then . . . was it true?

Ivan and Sergei thought so; Count Dubinksy was positive she was the grand duchess.

If only she could remember something of her former life. Of course, she'd read all about the Romanovs and had been moved by their tragic story. But how could a person *not* be moved? When she looked at photos of the family, all she saw was how brightly their affection for one another shone on their faces. Even when they were not smiling, their body language— the way they leaned toward one another or clasped hands—spoke volumes about their shared love.

Nadya sat up in bed, resting her forehead on her bent knees. *Think!* she urged herself. *There must be something you can remember from before the asylum. Think!*

Nothing. It was as though a wall existed in her mind, and behind it was everything she wanted to remember. She could almost feel the memories like flickering forms moving on the other side of the mental barrier, but she had no idea how to reach them.

Maybe her dreams were the answer, were the way around or through the wall of amnesia. Nadya reviewed her most memorable dreams. What had she seen? A sea of ink, the Black Sea; she could not recall ever having been to the Black Sea, but perhaps she had. She'd dreamed of Rasputin, though that didn't mean she'd met him; she might have seen his photo in a newspaper or book. The czarina Alexandra had appeared in her dreams. Here again, Nadya had seen her photograph, and it was natural enough to conjure these images from her more recent recollections.

Nadya recalled the frightening dreams of the man with the scar. She'd dreamed of him twice now. Back at the train station, his greedy glare had terrified her. Maybe he simply leered at young women. It also was possible he had come to represent all that scared her.

It was maddening not to know if her dreams were fabrications concocted from old newspaper stories and photographs or if they were a window into her old life.

The rumble of a motorcar interrupted the stillness of the morning, growing ever louder as it traveled up the count's long front drive. Why would someone be visiting this early?

Curious, Nadya slid out of bed and parted the curtains. Her room faced the front of the estate, and she could see a luxurious black Rolls Royce pulling up to the front steps. A uniformed chauffeur emerged and went to the front door. Nadya didn't hear a bell ring or a knocker bang. Was someone below expecting his arrival?

Nadya still was gazing out the window, pondering the visitor, when someone knocked on her door. "Are you awake?" Irina asked.

Nadya quickly opened the door to face Irina, who was wrapped in a thick robe. She was flushed with breathless excitement.

"What's going on?" Nadya asked her.

"The empress Marie has heard about you all the way in Paris," Irina reported. "She has sent her driver to bring you, Sergei, and Ivan to her. You must come right away."

"Right now?" Nadya questioned.

Irina flew into the room and pulled a suitcase from the closet. "Yes! Yes! Take this bag and throw in all the new things we bought. Oh, it's so lucky we went shopping! I suggest you put on the blue silk traveling suit. It's divine on you! But no, maybe it's too warm. It wouldn't be good to perspire; no doubt you'll be nervous enough when you meet the empress. Try that darling emerald-green sheath with the cap sleeves instead."

Nadya felt oddly unable to move. They'd thought of nothing but this for so long, but now it seemed to be happening much too quickly. It wasn't real somehow.

Irina swirled around her like a cyclone, tossing all Nadya's new things into the bag. "There, all packed!"

Nadya grabbed her grimy pillowcase satchel and tossed its contents into the suitcase, on top of her new outfits.

"Ah!" Irina cried. "Don't do that! Don't be offended, but those things are disgusting. Leave them here with me. I'll have them burned!"

As Nadya picked up the contents of the pillowcase, she noticed one of Sergei's white shirts. Three men's socks were in there also, each one a different color. "Oh dear," she sighed, realizing she had other things of Sergei and Ivan's as well. "We grabbed everything so fast when your brother's men came that we just threw everything together. I can't leave these things; they might need them."

Irina dumped one of the bed pillows from its case and laid the clean pillowcase on top of Nadya's new clothing. "At least separate the new things from that mess," she suggested kindly.

"Thanks," Nadya said, laying the old items on top.

"Now get dressed! Dowager Grand Empress Marie Feodorovna Romanov is not a woman to keep waiting!"

Nadya sat in the back of the Rolls Royce between Ivan and Sergei as they headed toward Paris. They'd been on the road for five hours and it was nearly noon. Ivan was talking to the driver, who also spoke Russian, explaining that none of them had the proper papers for entering France. The driver confidently told him not to worry. He knew what roads to take to avoid the government officials, and if they should be stopped, there were tried and true ways to get around even that. Nadya assumed these ways involved large sums of money.

"You're ready for this, you know," Sergei assured her. "You were spectacular at the party." He'd complimented her on her performance before, but he seemed to know she needed to hear it again.

"If she does accept me as Anastasia, how will it be?" she asked.

"It will be good," Sergei replied, patting her hand. "I have heard from reliable sources that the empress favored Anastasia above all her other grandchildren. You will be reunited with someone who loves you dearly. You will live luxuriously."

"As I once lived," she murmured.

"Yes, before the Revolution."

"Is it right to live that way, with so much wealth, when others are struggling as we have been struggling?" she asked him, scowling reflectively.

"That is a big question," Sergei commented. "But think of it this way. If you have wealth at your command, you will be in a position to help others."

"Did the Romanovs use their wealth to help others?"

"They had charities they contributed to and worked for," he replied.

"But did they do enough? Apparently the people of Russia didn't think so, or else they wouldn't have been overthrown, would they?"

"I don't know," Sergei admitted.

"Just take the money and don't worry about it," said Ivan, who had finished talking to the driver and had joined their conversation. "The old woman has enough of it, and she'll be happy to spend it on you."

"You know, I'm not doing this for the money," she said. "I have nobody in the world, no family, no friends. If I could recover my past and find my real grandmother, then maybe I could feel like I belonged, instead of like a piece of fluff being blown by every breeze."

"We're your friends," Ivan muttered, barely audible.

Despite the low tone, Nadya heard him. To her surprise, his words brought tears to her eyes. "I know that's true," she agreed in a voice choked with emotion. "And I haven't had friends before, not ones I can remember. Maybe we should turn back."

"Why?" Sergei asked.

"I don't know what's going to happen and I'm frightened," she told them.

"It's going to be all right," Ivan said. "Really."

Nadya nodded to be agreeable but was not convinced. This formidable dowager empress was a stranger to her. Maybe she was as austere as her grand title implied. Why should she trade these two true friends, one of whom she was deeply in love with—despite her reluctance to admit it—for a strict old aristocrat?

But Empress Marie *could* be her grandmother. A grandmother could fill in the blanks of her former life. A grandmother would be able to restore the memories that had once been hers. A grandmother could give her back her life. Nadya would no longer have that lingering sense that she was nobody at all, that she was a shadow or even a ghost.

This was the awful emptiness that she hated. If anything could take away that terrible fear and pain, it would be worth the risk.

CHAPTER NINETEEN
The Dowager Empress Marie

Ivan's stomach clenched as the driver stopped the car at the high iron gates surrounding the empress Marie's estate on the outskirts of Paris. The motor idled while a groundskeeper unbolted the lock.

This was it—the journey's end, the culmination of months of planning, searching, and traveling. Nadya had fallen asleep with her head on Sergei's shoulder. Sergei also slumbered, his head resting on the back of the seat.

The groundskeeper pulled open the gate, and the automobile proceeded up the drive. The empress's manor house was not a palace, but it possessed the same grandeur, only on a much smaller scale. More than a hundred years earlier, Ivan reflected, the French had revolted against this disparity between the starving lives of the poor and the lush lives of the rich. Yet what had it actually accomplished if places like this still existed?

It doesn't matter, he told himself harshly. He'd buried the idealist in himself, the one who was bothered by such things, and it was best if he stayed underground. There was no room for him in Ivan's plans.

Ivan's focus now was on playing his cards right, on staying smart and not letting emotion knock him off his game.

He reached across and jostled Nadya's shoulder. "Wake up. We're here."

Sergei sputtered awake, looking confused and then disappointed. "I dreamed I was home with Elana and my son, Peter."

Nadya rubbed his arm sympathetically.

At the wide, curved front steps, the driver opened the car door for them to get out. A butler in tuxedo tails met them and led the way to the front door. Inside the elegant white foyer with its rich blue-and-pink Persian rugs and ornately golden-framed mirrors, the butler bid them wait while he announced their arrival to the empress. "Remember, your name is Anastasia," Ivan whispered once the butler had gone.

"Yes, but I'll tell her I had forgotten it until recently," Nadya whispered back. "Otherwise I know I'll slip and forget."

"No," Ivan objected.

"Yes," Sergei insisted. "It's too late to switch her name now. It will look like we're trying to fool the empress if Nadya hesitates over the name Anastasia."

Ivan shot Sergei a meaningful glance. They *were*

trying to fool the empress, but they couldn't say that in front of Nadya.

"I'm so nervous," Nadya said with a tremble in her voice.

"You just be yourself and answer honestly," said Sergei.

"Let me do the talking," Ivan advised. He realized he had been snapping his fingers and he stopped abruptly. This would be the big moment. He was more anxious about it than he wanted to admit, even to himself.

The butler returned and gestured for them to follow him down the hall. He opened white doors with golden inlays, which led into a large room. A frail, elderly woman sat behind an impressive mahogany desk. Her still-thick white hair was piled high on her head, and what must have once been a pair of piercing blue eyes now cast a cataract-clouded gaze on them. "Come closer," the woman snapped in a brittle tone.

Ivan summoned the smooth charm he knew was his to command and made a sweeping bow. "Your Highness, it is an honor."

Sergei also bowed. But a sidelong glance told Ivan that Nadya simply was standing there as if dumbfounded. He fought the urge to poke her into a curtsy. Straightening, he smiled warmly at the empress. "Your Majesty, it is my great joy to introduce to you a young woman whom Count Kremnikov and I, Ivan Ivanovitch Navgorny, are convinced beyond all doubt to be your granddaughter, the grand duchess Anastasia Nicholaevna Romanov."

The empress hit her cane against the floor, and Ivan unintentionally jumped at the unexpected bang. Sergei and Nadya both flinched. "I know all that, you blathering fool!" she barked. "Did you not hear me? I said come closer! Let me see the girl."

Without Ivan's prompting, Nadya crossed the room and stood before the old woman. "Do you recognize me?" she asked, in a touching tone throbbing with need.

"My eyes are no longer sharp," replied the empress. "Lean in. Let me smell you."

Alarm washed over Nadya's face and for a second, Ivan was sure she would run. But she bent toward the empress, who inhaled and then waved her hand dismissively. "Nothing. Too much time has passed, perhaps. The scent of your skin is not familiar to me."

"Can you see me at all?" Nadya inquired.

"You're blurred," the woman replied. "But there is a quality in your voice reminiscent of the czarina Alexandra."

Ivan realized he had never heard the grand duchess speak in his time at the castle, nor had he heard the czarina.

"Tell me, were your mother and I close?" Empress Marie tested.

"I don't know," Nadya replied without hesitating. "If I ever knew, I have forgotten everything that happened before the day I awoke in an insane asylum."

Alarms sounded in Ivan's head. What was she doing? They had agreed not to mention that!

"Insane asylum?" the empress echoed, pulling back with distaste.

The whole story tumbled from Nadya's lips without artifice, complete with her desperate time living on the streets and the squalor of The Happy Comrades. "I had intended to spare you some of these details, but I so desire to be honest with you. I need to be candid and have nothing held back between us."

"Amnesia, eh?" said the empress. "Convenient."

Ivan felt he should intercede. "Maybe so, but it is quite understandable considering all she's been through. Wouldn't you agree?"

Ignoring him, Empress Marie turned her attention to Sergei and gruffly beckoned for him to approach her. "Count Kremnikov, have we met before?" she asked, narrowing her eyes to peer at him.

Sergei stepped forward. "Once, Your Majesty, at an affair of state. I was there with my mother and father. It was more than ten years ago."

The elderly dowager nodded. "But I have heard your named mentioned, and fairly recently too."

"Perhaps in the reports that reached your Imperial Highness regarding the grand duchess," Sergei suggested.

"Perhaps," she conceded. "I can't quite recall at this moment. It will come back to me eventually."

"So you agree that memory is a capricious faculty,"

Ivan said, seeing an opportunity to make his case.

Empress Marie glowered at him. "I am not a doddering idiot, young man. The elderly routinely struggle with lapses in memory, but complete amnesia is a rare condition. I am conversant with the new science of psychology and have read that memory can be buried in the unconscious or subconscious mind. It is not a usual occurrence, however, despite the unrealistic regularity with which the disease appears in contemporary fiction."

"All that you say is so," he agreed, "but it is an authentic condition nonetheless."

"Undoubtedly," she allowed with reluctant terseness.

The old bat isn't exactly the dusty relic I expected, he observed. The sharper her mind and senses, the less likely she'd be to accept Nadya without close scrutiny.

The empress turned her attention back to Nadya. "So you have no idea whether your mother and I were close?"

Nadya shook her head.

Try to at least guess! Ivan thought, frustrated with her passivity.

"Most of the girls who have come through here claiming to be my granddaughter have said that yes, we were very close. I knew instantly that they were fakes," the empress said.

"There have been others?" Nadya asked, shocked by the news.

"Oh yes," the empress confirmed with a bitter chuckle, "many others. I eventually exposed all of them as phonies, though some really had me going for a while, I must confess. Rest assured that I am battle weary in this endeavor, my girl, and disinclined to believe anyone."

"Then why did you send for me?" Nadya asked.

"People I trust were at the party last night. They are convinced you really are my Anastasia. Now that we've met, I will say that I find your voice compelling, but I need more than that before I am absolutely convinced. And this amnesia confuses the issue. How can I ask you to make me confident of your identity when you want *me* to confirm your past for you?"

Ivan had to admit, he could appreciate the old woman's quandary. If Nadya hadn't actually had amnesia, he never would have come up with such a story. The empress was right; the fact made things more difficult for her.

"You have put me in an odd predicament. I am suspicious that you simply may be three very savvy con artists who have twisted things more cleverly than those who lied to me outright," the empress continued.

"I have no memory of being Anastasia or anyone else," Nadya said candidly. "All I know is that Sergei and Ivan believe I am your granddaughter. Count Dubinsky also was sure of it. If I am not Anastasia, then I sincerely apologize for raising your hopes. I would never want to cause you more pain than you have already endured and—"

"What do you know of my pain?" The empress cut her off harshly. "You are a slip of a girl and know nothing of life."

"I know enough," Nadya shot back with fire, unabashed. "I have seen things you could never imagine; I know a kind of life that never makes its way over your high walls."

The empress Marie sat back in her chair and studied Nadya seriously. "It's been like that, has it?" she murmured gently.

Nadya turned away, averting her eyes to the ceiling. Ivan had seen the move before, an attempt to keep tears from spilling over. "Forgive me if I have offended you," Nadya implored with an unsteady voice.

"You will stay here with me," Empress Marie commanded. "Your friends may return for the weekend, at which time I will give you my decision and let them know if they can claim their reward."

Nadya's head snapped around and she stared at Ivan, wide-eyed with outrage. "There's a reward?"

In Nadya's eyes he saw himself reflected as a betrayer, a user, a liar, and a con artist. The hurt on her face left him speechless.

Chapter Twenty
Betrayed!

Nadya refused to look at Ivan and Sergei as they left the estate. Had all this been a scheme to win a reward?

That was certainly the way it appeared.

How could she have been so naive? So incredibly gullible? She had come to believe them completely. What a fool she'd been to think they were acting out of love for Mother Russia—and out of their concern for *her!*

If she had known it was a confidence game, a sham, she'd never have left Russia with them. Just the same, they hadn't even had the decency to let her in on their plan. And here she'd thought they were her best friends.

Ha! What a laugh!

But she was not amused.

Nadya now was alone with the empress in a lavishly ornate dining room. Swirling, vine-patterned wallpaper covered everything—even the ceiling—and was reflected in the gilded mirrors. Huge oil paintings depicted exotic flowers, orchids and other tropical plants she'd never even dreamed of. A long, gleaming, polished wood table reflected it all. She might as well have been trapped in a terrarium; this all was so strange to her. What was she supposed to do now?

"That little act was nearly convincing," Empress Marie said from her seat at the head of the table.

"What act?" Nadya asked, surprised by the remark.

"Pretending not to know about the reward."

"It wasn't an act. I didn't know."

The old woman's lips tightened into a cynical sneer. "You thought those two brought you all the way from Yekaterinburg to Paris out of the goodness of their hearts?"

Feeling foolish, Nadya nodded. "They told me they were doing it out of loyalty to the Romanovs."

The empress sighed. Nadya heard a deep weariness in it that she related to, despite the gulf in their ages. It made her think about how the world took so much out of a person. "I was stupid and naive to believe that, I know," Nadya conceded.

"*Young* and naive," the empress amended. "Or perhaps I have simply grown old and cynical. There certainly are those who laid down their lives fighting in the White Army for the Imperial Family. Many also joined to protect their status under the old regime, of course, but others fought out of sheer loyalty. The friends who smuggled me out of Siberia did so at great risk."

"Why didn't the whole family leave with you?" Nadya asked.

The empress rose, clearly agitated by the memories Nadya's question had evoked. "I begged Niki to leave with me, or to at least let me take the children. But he would never desert his people. He was so sure they would support him in the end. And he couldn't bear for them to hear that the family had fled."

"He was loyal to his people," Nadya noted.

The old woman angrily rapped the table with her fist. "What good is loyalty if it costs you everything you love?" Red-faced with emotion, she turned to Nadya. "A maid will bring you to your guest room. I must retire now. This interview has exhausted me."

"As you wish, Your Highness," Nadya said, bowing her head.

Empress Marie hobbled from the room, leaning heavily on her cane. The moment the empress was gone, Nadya wilted into a dining room chair and dropped her head into her hands. She understood how the empress felt: emotionally drained. How ironic, though, that an excess of memory had overwhelmed the old woman, whereas Nadya was feeling undone by a complete lack of the same.

If only she could remember something! Anything!

Nadya would welcome any memory, even one that proved she was *not* Anastasia, if only it would reveal a clue about who she *was*. Not knowing was driving her mad.

A maid in a black uniform with a white apron

entered the room. Nadya jumped up, embarrassed. Speaking in French, the maid entreated Nadya to follow her up the wide stairs in the center foyer to a guest room on the second floor. There, the suitcase she'd borrowed from Irina lay in the center of a four-poster bed.

When the maid had left, Nadya undid the latch and lifted out her belongings. At first, she wasn't sure where to set down the items. Every surface in the room was so clean and refined that she feared her things would stain them. Attached to her room was a white marble bathroom. The bathtub seemed the best place to deposit the items.

Returning to the suitcase, she continued to unpack, hanging her new dresses and suits in an ornately carved wardrobe. She recalled how happy Sergei had been when he'd handed her the German marks for shopping. At the time she'd thought him so generous, the best friend she could ever hope for. Now it made her so sad to understand it was just an investment to win him the much larger reward from the empress.

Once Nadya had unpacked, she went into the bathroom to sort through her old belongings. Undoubtedly Irina had been right when she'd said most of it should be burned. But before destroying her old clothing, she'd have to pick out the men's garments she'd hastily snapped up and, of course, put aside her little doll.

But as she picked through the clothing, it slowly dawned on her that her little cloth doll was not there.

With mounting panic, Nadya shuffled the items in the tub, raking her mind to recall the last time she'd seen the doll. She could picture it lying on the blanket near the spent fire at the campsite in Germany. She'd thought she'd tossed it into the bundle when they'd left. She didn't remember seeing it after that, but it had been the last thing on her mind as she'd packed to meet the empress. Could she have dropped it when they went up to Count Dubinsky's estate?

The deep pang of loss she experienced made her feel childish. It was nothing, really, and she tried to put aside thoughts of the doll.

But it had been with her for so long. Many times it had been her only friend.

With a gasp, she swallowed a gulp of air. Her eyes were wet. How strange that such a small thing could affect her so deeply.

Suddenly, Nadya was incredibly weary from her long car ride from Germany and all that had happened afterward. She wanted nothing more than to escape the waking world, at least for a while. Throwing herself on top of the bed, she stretched out and let her heavy eyelids slide shut.

She is back in the bedroom with the four cots lined up in a row. Nadya is holding a star in her hand. No, not a star: A very large diamond. Empress Marie enters. "What have you got there, my sweet?" she asks in a kind voice very unlike the one Nadya has heard her use today.

Nadya is outside herself, watching another, younger Nadya.

"Mother wanted to give away her Marie Antoinette necklace to Father Grigory," this younger Nadya tells the empress, lifting the diamond to show her. "Count Dubinsky and Prince Yuperov wouldn't let her. They fought over the necklace and it broke. This fell out but they didn't notice it. I was here, watching. Other diamonds fell too, but somehow they missed this one when they were picking up the others."

Empress Marie takes the diamond. "That foolish, foolish woman," she comments softly.

"I should bring it to Mother."

"Don't worry. I will bring it to her. Go to the sewing room. I have had special petticoats made for you and your sisters. You are not to tell anyone this, not ever. It will be our secret. There are jewels sewn into the waistbands of these special petticoats."

"But what good are jewels if no one can see them?" Nadya asks. "Isn't the fun of jewelry to show it off?"

"These are dangerous times, my pet," Empress Marie says in a serious but gentle tone. "The hidden jewels are like insurance. Guards can be bribed. Favors may be purchased."

"Will we need to do those things?"

"I pray not. Perhaps someday you will use the jewels to build your own fine summer palace like the one your parents have overlooking the Black Sea," she says. She smiles fondly. "Go now so the seamstresses can be sure your petticoat fits before they sew the finishing touches."

"Should I tell Mother you have this missing diamond?" Nadya asks.

"No," Empress Marie says. "Do not tell your mother anything. Let it be our secret for now. I will take care of it."

"You're sure we're doing the right thing, Grandmother?" Nadya checked.

"Absolutely, my darling," the empress said, stroking her cheek tenderly. "Don't bother yourself about it any further."

Nadya awoke on the pink-and-blue bedspread, mentally clutching at the few fragments of the dream that she could recall—the gentle voice, the luminous diamond, the ominous feeling that an unnamed, invisible danger was silently mounting around her.

Sitting upright, it occurred to her that she was now in a position to ask someone who might know why she was having the dream: the empress Marie.

As Nadya got up off the bed, she checked the clock on the night table. It was just a little after five. Maybe the empress was up from her nap. Nadya had so many questions for her.

Nadya stepped out of her room into the quiet hallway and down the grand central staircase. As she descended, she scanned the foyer for a servant to ask for the empress's whereabouts but saw no one. On the first floor she checked the large room where they'd first spoken and then the dining room. They were both empty.

Moving farther down the hallway, Nadya went

through an archway leading into a library. There she found the empress seated on a velvet couch in the center of the room. Empress Marie was slumped to the side, but her gentle snores assured Nadya that she was merely napping.

A scrapbook of photos lay open on the empress's lap. Coming behind the couch, Nadya peered down at them. Four lovely blond girls sat together with a much younger boy in the middle.

The face of the youngest girl riveted her to the page. No wonder Ivan had wanted her for this scheme of his! The resemblance was incredible, although the face of the girl in the photo was fuller and younger.

Anastasia's eyes sparkled, completely lacking the haunted expression Nadya sometimes had noted on her own face. Nonetheless, there was an uncanny similarity.

Below that photo was another picture of the same group, smiling and skating on a frozen pond with the huge palace looming behind them. Coats lined in ermine and full fur hats and muffs kept the girls warm. With them was a man she recognized from news photos as Czar Nicholas. How happy they all appeared!

On the opposite page were two formal photos, one of Nicholas and one of Alexandra. Nadya could see that Anastasia strongly resembled her mother. Curious to see more, she reached across the empress's shoulder and turned the page.

Nadya gasped sharply and drew back as if she'd been stung!

The fiery eyes of Grigory Rasputin stared up at her from the photograph. He stood beside the czar and czarina. And on the other side of Rasputin was the man who had frightened her at the train station— the one with the terrible twisted scar.

CHAPTER TWENTY-ONE
A Showdown

From their Paris hotel room, Ivan looked down at the lush and colorful Luxembourg Gardens. His dark mood made it impossible for him to appreciate its bounty of spring blooms. Instead, he scowled out at the sunny day.

Turning from the window, Ivan cast a desultory glance at Sergei, who lay on his bed, hands behind his head, staring at the ceiling. "Look at us!" Ivan cried. "What a pair of mutts we are! We've almost achieved our goal. Why are we acting like this?"

"You know why," Sergei replied. "We should have told Nadya the truth about the reward."

"She'd never have come with us."

"It was wrong not to tell her. And what if that sharp-tongued old lady doesn't believe she's Anastasia?" Sergei asked, sitting up. "She'll be in a foreign country where she knows no one and has no papers. At least back in Russia she had a job and a place to live."

"You call what she was doing there living?"

"Don't avoid the subject."

"The old bat isn't going to reject her," Ivan insisted. "You heard the empress. She sounds like her mother the czarina. *Sounds* like her! When I heard that, I couldn't believe it. What luck! Who would have expected that?"

"And you're still convinced that she's not Anastasia?" Sergei questioned.

"Yes, I'm convinced. Nadya might be some aristocrat's lost daughter, but she's not the grand duchess Anastasia."

"Why not?" Sergei pressed.

"Firstly, I saw her get shot. Secondly, how likely is it that we decide to find a girl to play Anastasia and discover the real grand duchess?"

"Look at it a different way," Sergei suggested. "We set out to find the grand duchess because rumors were circulating that she was still alive. The rumors turned out to be true and we did, in fact, succeed in finding her."

Ivan waved him away. It was too preposterous!

"It's possible," Sergei said.

Ivan threw up his arms, vexed by Sergei's insistence. "No, it's not possible! I will tell you why I am sure beyond all doubt that Nadya is not Anastasia."

"I'm listening. Why?"

"You saw her last night in that strapless dress?"

"Yes. She was breathtaking in it."

"I watched Anastasia Romanov get hit right in the chest with a bullet. Even if some surgeon worked a miracle and saved her life . . . there would be a scar."

Sergei nodded thoughtfully, considering Ivan's words. "You're right," he admitted. "There was no scar."

"No scar," Ivan echoed.

"That's good, I suppose. At least now we are sure we really are perpetrating a most outrageous swindle," Sergei said quietly. "There is nothing uncertain about it."

"We never set out to hurt anyone," Ivan argued. "Why should I feel badly about that?"

"Because it was dishonest right from the start."

Ivan opened his mouth to protest, and then he slowly shut it as he felt the weight of Sergei's words. Ivan settled thoughtfully into an armchair, tapping the tips of his fingers together and trying to reconcile his swirling emotions with the facts.

What was he feeling?

Guilt?

Guilt was an emotion he loathed, but it was undeniably there. He could rationalize his actions for a hundred years and still it would not erase the raw look of betrayal he'd seen in Nadya's eyes.

Shame?

He *was* ashamed of having deceived her about his true intentions. There was no sense in denying it.

There was another emotion lurking just below those two. Ivan rubbed his face with both hands, frustrated that he could not name it.

"You're afraid of losing her, aren't you?" Sergei suggested gently. "She loves you too, you know."

Ivan dropped his head in despair. "What should I do, Sergei?"

"It seems to me that you must be perfectly honest with her. Share your thoughts and your feelings with her."

"No. I can't. If Empress Marie believes she is Anastasia, how can I rob her of that future?"

"Would life with you be so terrible?" Sergei asked.

"I am not a rich man, even if I do collect a reward."

"I believe that when I find my Elana, she will still love me, even though I am no longer a wealthy aristocrat."

Ivan concentrated on keeping his face immobile. He didn't want even the slightest facial expression to betray his true feelings about what Sergei had just said. The chances that Elana and Peter were still alive were very slim, in his estimation. Otherwise, why wouldn't someone have heard from them? Ivan knew that Sergei would never give up the search for his wife and son, though. Ivan did not have the heart to convince his friend otherwise.

"That's different," Ivan said evenly. "You two are already a devoted couple. Nadya and I haven't even really begun. Why start something that can't be finished?"

"Because you love each other."

Ivan stood and went back to the window. "Sergei, you're a romantic fool," he snapped, continuing to scowl.

"You should write her a letter. Tell her how you feel," Sergei suggested.

Ivan considered this. Perhaps his friend was right. Then she would know his feelings for her had been real, and though it was not his desire for them to be kept apart, he knew he was helpless in the face of her grand destiny.

Ivan sighed. Whether she was Anastasia or not, he felt sure that somehow it was Nadya's fate to live out her life as the grand duchess. Every bit of his gut intuition told him that the empress would believe Nadya really was her granddaughter. Somehow, he just knew it.

"Do you still have that ink?" he asked Sergei.

"Not much, most of it spilled. What's left is in my bag. Help yourself."

Sergei's bag sat open on his bed. Rummaging through, Ivan pulled out Nadya's ink-stained old white petticoat. "What's this?" he asked, holding it up to Sergei.

"Nadya's petticoat. We used it as a rag when the ink spilled," Sergei replied. "When Count Dubinsky's men came to get us, everything got tossed together."

Ivan noticed the scorched bullet tears in the waistband. Turning over the fabric, he saw another hole in the bodice of the petticoat.

Suddenly his blood felt like ice. Gooseflesh rose on his arms. "Did you see this?" he asked.

"Yes, they look like bullet holes, don't they?" Sergei answered. "They gave her that petticoat in the asylum."

"What if they didn't?" Ivan asked with mounting excitement.

"I don't follow."

"I've heard stories that there were jewels sewed into the petticoats that the grand duchesses wore."

Sergei arose and came to Ivan's side to reexamine the petticoat. "I didn't know that," he said.

"It wasn't something the soldiers wanted generally known, because they stole the jewels. But they bragged about it to the other soldiers."

Sergei visibly shuddered with repulsion.

"It's unbelievable," he murmured. "I *saw* her die. See this hole?" Ivan showed Sergei the tear in the bodice. "Anastasia was shot in the chest. But it's impossible."

Sergei put a hand on Ivan's shoulder. "Apparently not."

"It *is* impossible," Ivan insisted. "Remember . . . Nadya has no scar."

That evening, Ivan ate supper alone in an outdoor café on the Left Bank of the city. The weather was warm with a gentle breeze. The last light of the lengthening spring day threw a soft cast over the bustling city.

Filled with nervous energy, he absentmindedly tapped on the coffee cup in front of him. Had he really found Anastasia? Ivan laughed softly to himself, shaking his head and marveling at the sheer improbability of it.

How had she done it? She'd been utterly trapped there in the forest. He had seen them shoot her as she'd tried to escape.

That he couldn't reconcile. He was sure the bullet had hit her squarely in the chest. It should have been a fatal shot to the heart.

That petticoat, though . . . not only was it bullet-ridden, but he'd seen it before. There had to be other petticoats like it . . . but still . . . Anastasia had been wearing just such an undergarment; he'd seen it beneath her torn dress.

From his pocket, Ivan took out her small rag doll. Sergei had found it with the petticoat. Ivan had it on him now with the intention of returning it to Nadya. He knew it was only an excuse to visit her. The truth was, he missed her already.

Ivan paid his bill, and then he hailed a cab to take him over a bridge, across the darkly flowing Seine River that ran through Paris, and to the wealthier Right Bank. He had the driver continue on until they were nearly out of the city, in the more suburban section. He got out at the empress's gated estate.

He convinced the groundskeeper to admit him through the gates but, at the front door, the butler reported that Nadya would not see him. Ivan was turning to leave when a sudden intuition redirected him. He hurried along the side of the estate until he came to a well-manicured garden, with flowing fountains and paved paths.

As he'd hoped, Nadya was there. She sat on a bench beneath a row of flowering cherry trees, looking at a book. The slightest breeze sent a shower of pink blossoms raining down on her, catching in her hair and in the folds of her clothing. She was so engrossed in her reading that she didn't appear to notice.

Ivan approached her quietly, thinking that she looked every inch a princess, but not even an earthly one. Sitting there, so utterly transported by her reading, with the cherry blossoms blowing around her and the last of the light outlining her short blond waves, she struck him as having the radiance and otherworldly beauty of a princess from a fairy tale.

A twig snapped under Ivan's foot and Nadya looked up sharply, her head turning toward the sound. Her eyes narrowed with hostile suspicion when she saw him. "What do you want?" she demanded coldly.

"To explain."

"Oh, I don't think that's necessary," she scoffed with a cynical chuckle. "It's all pretty clear to me."

"Maybe it's not what you think," he suggested as he sat beside her on the bench. He saw she had been perusing a photo album filled with photographs of the Romanovs.

"I *think* that you deceived me to con a rich old woman into giving you a reward. How's that? Fairly accurate?"

"Completely accurate," he admitted grimly. "At

least that's how it started, but along the way things changed."

"What things?"

"My feelings for—"

"What feelings?" she cried, standing. "You have no feelings! If you mean the romantic charade you've been performing to entertain yourself and to pump up that huge male ego of yours, *those* aren't feelings. I admit I fell for it at first but I see through it now, thank you very much!"

Ivan was at a turning point. He knew he could go one of two ways. He'd been on the verge of confessing his love for Nadya when she'd interrupted him. Her volatile outburst had presented him with another path, however.

If he had ever loved her, the feeling was never more overpowering than at this moment. She was so vulnerable, yet so strong in her anger. But if he loved her, he could not snatch away this new life from her. What kind of shallow, self-serving love would that be?

To conceal his true feelings—as Ivan had almost done—would not be an act of love. He knew Nadya could be impulsive and emotional. He felt sure she loved him too, and so she would toss everything else aside for love. It was how she was—and he couldn't let her do it.

"You're right," he said, ridding his voice of warmth. "It's a hobby of mine; I like to see if I can get every girl I meet to fall for me. At first, you were such an ungodly mess I wasn't interested, but as you got better-looking along the way, you began to pique my interest."

Nadya's mortified expression made Ivan inwardly cringe, but he kept on. It would be better if she hated him; it would give him less of a chance to lose his resolve and beg her to come away with him. "Now I can add you to the list of my successes," he added.

Ivan's head snapped back as she slapped him hard across the face.

Mission accomplished, he thought with bitter irony as he rubbed his fiery cheek.

Tears racing down her cheeks, Nadya grabbed the photograph album from the bench and ran toward the estate, disappearing through a back door.

Ivan fought the impulse to go after her.

Instead, he headed back to the front gate and got the groundskeeper to let him out. He'd given no thought to how he'd get back to his hotel, but it didn't matter. He wanted to walk a while anyway.

CHAPTER TWENTY-TWO
The Story Unfolds

Nadya clutched the photo album to her heaving chest as she stood in a dimly lit back hallway and allowed her tears to flow freely. What a truly terrible day this had turned out to be. She had been betrayed; her beloved doll was gone; even her meeting with the empress had not been the warm reunion she had hoped for. And now these awful, cruel words from Ivan!

Only the night before, her future had seemed full of hope. She was dancing in Ivan's arms, accepted by the guests and about to be reunited with her grandmother. How had things all gone wrong so quickly?

The empress stepped into a doorway at the end of the hall, leaning heavily on her cane. "I thought I heard something," she said. Quickly looking Nadya up and down, she realized her miserable state. "Are you crying? What's wrong?"

"I just fought with Ivan," Nadya admitted.

"Are you two in love?" the empress asked with the bluntness that Nadya was coming to realize was a hallmark of her personality.

"I thought we were. But it seems I was the only one in love."

Empress Marie nodded. "I see."

"I've been so stupid," Nadya said, wiping her eyes.

"Come closer so I can see you," the empress demanded.

When Nadya was beside her, Empress Marie noticed the photo album tucked under Nadya's arm. With a tightening brow, her eyes blazed angrily. "Where did you get that?"

Nadya reddened with embarrassment. "I'm sorry. It was open on your lap, and I started looking at it."

"How dare you!" the empress cried. "What did you hope to do, use what you learned in here to trick me?"

"No! Really, no!" Nadya insisted. "You were asleep, so I took the book to see if the photos would awaken any memories."

"And I suppose now you remember everything? Our life together in Russia, how lovely everything was, how you used to call me Granny," the empress said, her voice dripping with sarcasm.

Nadya shook her head. "No. Nothing came to me. I only felt sad that such a lovely family should have met so tragic an end."

The empress looked away sharply, as if studying something on the ceiling. When she turned back to Nadya, her eyes were rimmed in red. "Give me that book right now," the elderly woman barked fiercely.

Nadya moved to comply but then held back. "I must ask you about one photograph. Please, I need to know." Balancing the album on her hip, Nadya fumbled through to the page featuring the scarred man and held it up to the empress. "This man with the scar. Who is he?"

Empress Marie held her in an intense stare. "Why do you ask me that?"

"He was following me at the Trans-Siberian train station."

The empress gasped. "You saw him?"

"Yes, at the station."

"Then he's alive!"

Nadya nodded. "Who is he?"

"He was Rasputin's assistant, Lepski. Every bit as foul as his boss."

"Why have you kept his picture?"

"Because my Niki and Alexandra are in it. But I should cut those other two scoundrels out," she said. "You say he's been following you?"

"It seems that way. Do you know why?"

"Come into the library with me," she said with her hand held over her heart. "I need to sit. I will tell you what I know."

Empress Marie sat on the library couch with the album on her lap. Nadya settled into an upholstered chair across from her.

"Your mother loved . . ." Stopping, she scrutinized Nadya with narrowed eyes, assessing how to continue. "The czarina Alexandra," she amended, "loved her children very much, and she worried endlessly about Alexei's health. I don't know how he did it, but that devil Rasputin was the only one who seemed able to help him. This gave him tremendous influence with Alexandra. She gave him all sorts of gifts, but he was never satisfied."

"But if Rasputin could help, who could blame her?" Nadya sympathized.

"I understand, but she went too far," the empress said, shaking her head sadly. "Alexandra was a German princess, as was Marie Antoinette before she became the queen of France—another unfortunate victim of another bloody revolution. A priceless necklace that had once belonged to that ill-fated queen came to Alexandra through family lines. In a rash moment, when she was out of her mind with fear that Alexei would die, she promised it to Rasputin if he could cure the boy."

Nadya's hand crept to her throat as she listened in rapt silence. She did not fully remember her dreams, but she knew she had dreamed of a necklace of brilliant diamonds. "It was a diamond necklace?" she inquired quietly.

The empress was surprised. "How did you know?"

"I've dreamed of a diamond necklace. I think Rasputin and the czarina were in the dream."

"You've dreamed it? At night, while you slept?"

"Yes."

The empress's face softened for a moment before she tugged it back into stern lines. "The story was leaked briefly in the Russian newspapers before Niki had it suppressed. Perhaps you saw it. It ran with a drawing of the necklace."

"Perhaps I did," Nadya allowed. "It would have been from before the time I can remember."

"Well this insect, this Lepski, liked to drink, and when he was drunk he would brag that Rasputin was soon to come into possession of an invaluable heirloom. This story got to Prince Yuperov, who hated Rasputin with a passion—as did many others. It was he who eventually orchestrated Rasputin's execution. When he heard that Rasputin would get the necklace, he was outraged. He said it was state property, since Alexandra was the czarina of All the Russias. He intervened before Alexandra could hand over the necklace to Rasputin, and Niki took Yuperov's side in the argument."

As though jolted from her unconscious mind by Empress Marie's recollections, the images of this scene—the men and Alexandra struggling for the necklace—returned to Nadya. It made her nearly dizzy with emotion as she realized that she knew exactly what the empress was telling her, as though she had seen the whole thing.

This was no dream concocted from a newspaper report.

She had seen this!

"My son sided with Prince Yuperov and Count Dubinksy, who aided the prince. He denied Rasputin the necklace. This fellow Lepski was more incensed over Niki's decision than even Rasputin appeared to be. He swore revenge on the whole Romanov family if the necklace was not given over. Apparently Rasputin had promised him the diamonds from the bottom strand."

"Why did Prince Yuperov spare his life?" Nadya asked.

"Before they attempted to execute Rasputin, they got him drunk. Lepski was there and became so inebriated that he fell under the table. He was roused by the commotion during the struggle with Rasputin, and he crawled away."

"What became of the necklace?"

"No one knows," Empress Marie replied, but Nadya was sure she had detected a small catch in the woman's voice, a split second of hesitation. *No one else knows, perhaps,* she thought, *but you know, don't you?* She decided not to press the subject, even though she was sure the empress was lying. What was the point in antagonizing her?

Empress Marie studied Nadya with a direct gaze. "I wish my eyesight were better and I could see you clearly," she said. "But this Lepski obviously believes you are Anastasia. He saw the girl many times—to my great displeasure, let me add."

"You think that's why he's been following me?"

168

"Why else?" the empress questioned. "That has to be the reason."

"What would he want from me?"

"The same thing your friends want? The reward?" the empress suggested.

"They're no longer my friends," Nadya said strongly.

"You really did not know about the reward?" asked the empress incredulously.

"I swear to you, I didn't. I came with them because anything would have been better than where I was. I hoped they would help me find my lost family. I would be just as happy to find my grandmother if she lived in a run-down cottage in the country. I'm so tired of being lost and alone."

Empress Marie reached out her soft, bony hand and laid it on top of Nadya's hand. "I am too," she said.

As Nadya looked into the empress's eyes, she felt sure this was her grandmother. It was an instinct, a kind of blood recognition. But could she trust it? The feeling might be mere wishful thinking. "I wish I could tell you for certain who I am," she said honestly.

The empress nodded. "So do I." Setting aside the album, Empress Marie stood. "Put on your best evening outfit. We will dine at The Ritz, and then I will take you to the Paris Opera House. Tchaikovsky's opera Eugene Onegin, a fine Russian story, is being performed. Let's see what the other White Russians in Paris make of you."

CHAPTER TWENTY-THREE
The Scarred Man's Attack

So now it was done. Over between them. It was for the best. Ivan tried to convince himself of this as he followed the trail of the Seine River on his way back to the center of Paris.

Sergei and he had agreed that if by some chance the empress didn't believe she was Anastasia, they'd give Nadya what was left of Sergei's money. It was at least enough to buy a train ticket back to Yekaterinburg and for her to rent an apartment, though she'd probably do better to stay in Paris and look for work as a waitress or a maid since she had experience in those jobs.

What a choice that would be, he thought, *to be either a grand duchess or a maid.* There was nothing wrong with being a maid or a waitress; it was honest work. Nadya had worked hard before. She could do it again. But still . . .

The brilliant lights of Paris were illuminating the night sky by the time Ivan neared the center of town. The famed Eiffel Tower, fully lit, dominated the view. *How romantic it would be to share this sight with Nadya,* he thought and then quickly upbraided himself. *Be done with it once and for all. Stop thinking of her! You'll never again share anything together.*

Ivan was traveling along the Seine's stone-paved embankments. On his left was the black river with its shimmering reflections. On his right was a stone wall with steps that appeared at intervals, leading up to the sidewalk and street overhead. These steps also led to bridges that crossed the river, connecting the formal and expensive Right Bank, which he was on, with the more Bohemian, arty Left Bank, where he was headed.

Ever-quickening footsteps sounded an alert that someone was walking behind him. Glancing over his shoulder, Ivan saw no one—which meant someone had ducked into the shadow of the wall or was in the darkness under the last bridge he'd passed.

With every sense now hyperalert, Ivan continued on. Once again he detected footsteps.

Was he about to be robbed?

If Ivan could make it up a staircase to the street, it would be more public and safe. But he'd have to pass under another bridge before he got to the next set of steps. There he'd be hidden from the city's glowing lights: a perfect spot for a mugger to overtake him. Ivan could defend himself well enough if the attacker wasn't carrying a weapon, but that was a risk he preferred not to take. Better to stay in the illumination of the street lamps where, if he were attacked, he might be seen and receive some help from the street above.

Ivan walked on, slowing his steps. Then, abruptly, he stopped and turned quickly.

The man with the twisted scar faced him, a bowler hat pulled low over his eyes, his long black coat unnecessary in the warm night.

Ivan advanced aggressively toward him. "What do you want?" he demanded. "Why are you following me?"

"I want what was promised to me," the man growled. "I want the necklace."

"What necklace?"

"You know the one."

"I don't. You've followed me all the way from Russia for a necklace? Why would you think I have some necklace?"

"Because you have the girl," he snarled.

"Nadya?"

The scarred man's sniggering laugh reminded Ivan of every unsavory thing he'd ever known. "You know that's not her name," the scarred man insisted. He drew a small revolver from beneath his coat and pointed it at Ivan. "I was about to grab her myself, but you beat me to it. Hand over the necklace. I saw you come from the estate. I know you've collected the reward."

Ivan was curious as to what necklace the man was talking about, but the gun pointing at his chest made him disinclined to stand around discussing it. Instead, Ivan's instinct to survive trumped all other concerns.

Lowering his head, Ivan charged the man, butting him hard in the stomach with the crown of his own forehead.

The man grunted as the air was knocked from his lungs. With arms windmilling for balance, he staggered backward toward the Seine.

The earsplitting blast of his revolver cracked the night as the man toppled into the black golden-flecked river.

Ivan was thrown back against the wall by the force of the gunshot. Sliding down the wall, he rammed the palm of his hand into the wound in his chest to stem the gushing blood. With peering eyes, he tried to locate the man in the river, but he couldn't see anything but black and red before he lost consciousness.

CHAPTER TWENTY-FOUR
Revelations in the Night

Nadya sat with Empress Marie in her box seat in the balcony of the Paris Opera House. She leaned over and tapped the old woman's ring-laden hand to get her attention. "This music is so familiar," she whispered. "Would Anastasia have known it?"

The empress eyed her without emotion. "What do *you* think?"

"I don't know. But I've heard this before and not at The Happy Comrades."

"I daresay not," the empress said drily.

Turning to face front again, Nadya was aware that there was a buzz of interest sweeping the audience. With increasing frequency, heads turned around as people tried to steal a glimpse of her in the box. Several handsome young men caught her eye and waved. One even winked at her!

For the evening's event, Nadya had selected a

gown that was not as fancy as the one she'd worn to the previous night's party but that was elegant just the same. It was a floor-length, strapless black dress with a sheer black ruffle running across the top. She'd swept back her short hair with a jeweled hair band that the empress had loaned her for the evening, along with a fringed black shawl, to keep off any evening breeze, and elbow-length black gloves. Attired like this, Nadya felt beautiful and worldly.

What would the patrons of The Happy Comrades think if they could see her now? What would Mrs. Zolokov think? Oddly enough, Nadya's new role as an elegant lady did not feel alien to her. In fact, she felt strangely comfortable with her surroundings and her new appearance. When these flirty young men tried to get her attention, she felt confident enough to smile politely and then look away, knowing they would still be staring at her.

Nadya already had met a few of the men at dinner, where they had vied to sit near her. Finding a replacement for Ivan would be no problem among this group of exiled Russian aristocrats. They mostly were the sons of counts, dukes, barons, and princes.

At dinner she had sat between the empress and a plump Russian woman in a red dress, Baroness Kakofsky. "I heard from Irina Dubinsky that Count Kremnikov and a friend of his escorted your relative from Moscow," she'd said.

The empress had nodded. "Tell me, Baroness

Kakofsky, what is it I have heard about Count Krem-nikov lately? I simply can't remember. Can you?"

Baroness Kakofsky had thought but shook her head. "He *was* the subject of recent conversation, but I no longer can recall why," she'd replied and then twittered with laughter. "Last week's gossip always goes right out of my head. The new gossip simply sweeps it away." Tilting her head, she'd thought again. "Kremnikov was thought to be dead, wasn't he?"

"Was he?" the empress had countered, raising an eyebrow with interest.

"Someone named Kremnikov was supposedly dead, I seem to recall," the baroness had said with a shrug. "Oh well. I'll make inquiries and let you know."

Now Nadya sat at the opera, letting the strangely familiar music wash over her without really paying attention to the story. Instead, she focused on what life would be like as Anastasia Romanov, allowing herself to feel how good it all would be.

At intermission, Baroness Kakofsky hurried over to Nadya and the empress. "I've found the answer to your query," she reported excitedly. "Kremnikov's wife, Elana, and their son were spotted by someone over at the Cluny medieval monastery. I don't know who reported it, but the person said Elana believes Kremnikov is dead. She's quite penniless now, you know, but she's working for her keep over there."

"Elana is alive!" Nadya cried, gasping and stag-gering back a step. "I have to let Sergei know. Is there a telephone in this theater?"

"In the ticket office, perhaps," the empress suggested. "Is their hotel here on the Right Bank?"

Nadya shook her head. "I'm not sure." All she knew was that Ivan had said they would be staying at a hotel across from the Luxembourg Gardens.

"That's the Left Bank," said the baroness, "and it's not wired for telephone yet."

"Then I have to go there!"

"You don't even know where you're going," the empress pointed out.

"How many hotels can there be across from the Gardens?" Nadya asked.

"Quite a few," Baroness Kakofsky assured her.

Nadya already was backing away from them, heading for the door. "I'll find him. Don't worry."

"Have you cab fare?" Empress Marie asked, digging into her clutch bag.

"No, thank you," Nadya said, accepting the French francs. With the money bunched in her hand, she ran out front, where she found several idling taxis waiting to transport the operagoers. "Luxembourg Gardens, please," she requested as she slid into one of them.

"At this time of night?" the driver questioned.

"Please, just hurry," she urged him. All her anger and feelings of betrayal had flown when she heard this news about Sergei's wife and son. How could she stay angry with Sergei when he had been so kind? She could be indignant again tomorrow if she chose, but now it was more important that he know his family was close. If anyone knew the ache of being without one's family, it was Nadya.

It wasn't long before the driver pulled up to the Gardens. Paying him quickly, she hurried from the taxi into the nearest hotel. At the third hotel where she inquired, Nadya found Count Kremnikov and Ivan Navgorny listed in the register.

Hurrying into the wrought-iron lift, she took it to the fourth floor and was soon banging on Sergei and Ivan's door. "Hold on, Ivan," Sergei called from within. When Sergei opened the door, his face lit up with delighted surprise. "Nadya! How beautiful you look! I'm so happy to—"

She rushed in, grabbing his arm. "The Monastery de Cluny. The driver told me it's not very far from here." She pulled a scrap of paper from her glove on which she'd scribbled the directions the driver had given her. "Here, go here. Right now!"

"What's going on?" he asked, confused. "Is Ivan with you?"

"He came to see me but left at dusk," she replied, not wanting to relate the details of their bitter meeting.

"I hope nothing's happened to him," Sergei fretted.

"Oh, he's fine, just rude and thoughtless. No doubt he's out prowling the Parisian nightlife in search of a good time," she said.

"Possibly," Sergei allowed.

"But listen," she said. "You must go. I heard a rumor tonight. Elana and your son may be at the Cluny."

Sergei drew a sharp breath. "Who told you this?"

"A Russian woman named Baroness Kakofsky."

"That horrible old harpy! How does she know?"

"She heard it somewhere. That's the news that Empress Marie was trying to recall."

Sergei moved around the room as though not sure which way to head first. Nadya's words had thrown him off balance, as she had thought they might.

"Be careful not to come upon her too suddenly. Elana thinks you're dead," she warned him.

"*I'm* dead?"

"Go! Go to them," Nadya urged impatiently.

"I don't know if I'm ready," he fretted, raking his hands through his short hair in a frantic attempt to comb it.

Nadya scooped his velvet jacket off a chair and put it in his hands. "You're just nervous. Now go!" she said, pulling him toward the open door.

"Leave Ivan a note. Tell him where I've gone," Sergei called over his shoulder as he hurried down the hall, his pace increasing with every step.

"I will. Good luck!" Nadya shouted after him.

That's the difference between them, she thought with a sigh, watching Sergei disappear into the lift. *He doesn't want Ivan to worry, while Ivan couldn't care less about anyone but himself.*

Turning back to the room, Nadya searched for something to write with. The nearly dry jar of ink was on the desk, but she saw no paper. Surely the front desk would have some. Closing the door behind her, Nadya went down in the lift to ask. "I need some paper to write a note, please," she requested of the young clerk at the desk. "The note's to Mr. Navgorny in Room 410. If I leave it with you, would you give it to him when he comes in?"

The man's eyes darted to a paper on the desk in front of him. He said something to her in French.

"Pardon?" she inquired. "I don't speak your language."

He handed the paper he'd been looking at to Nadya. "*La police a apporté cet article,*" he said. "*Elle regarde n'ce importe qui qui pourrait connaître cet homme. Je pense que c'est Monsieur Navgorny.*"

Nadya looked down at the paper and gripped the desk in shock. It showed a sketch of a badly injured man lying on a table. Below it someone had quickly printed the name Ivan Navgorny.

CHAPTER TWENTY-FIVE
Elana Kremnikov

Sergei ran through the Gardens. He was so excited that it didn't occur to him to find a taxi. By the light of the moon and an occasional gas lamp, he maneuvered through the flower-lined pathways.

It was as though fate had brought him here to Paris. To think that Elana and Peter could be so close!

With a pounding heart, he stopped beneath a lamppost to reread the directions. They directed him to go around the Gardens; certainly running diagonally through them would be faster. Not a moment could be wasted. The need to see Elana and Peter again was so overpowering that Sergei felt as though he might explode with anticipation.

Out of the Gardens, Sergei turned the wrong way at first, and then realized his mistake. Correcting his course, he came to an ancient-looking stone building in the heart of the city. Its gated courtyard faced out onto the street. Yanking on the gate, Sergei discovered it was unlocked, and he entered.

Sergei made his way into the building through a wooden door that also was unlocked. He sent up a silent prayer of thanks that these monks were so trusting and welcoming.

Wavering shadows were thrown on the walls by candles that flickered in wall sconces. The dancing light magnified the shadows thrown by carved wooden statues of saints that stood on pedestals along the way.

From behind a door, Sergei heard a hypnotic chanting: monks in meditation. Cracking open the door, he peered into a chapel. A soft light was on its altar. Black-hooded monks knelt with their heads bowed. Sergei shut his eyes and let the calming ancient chanting sounds wash over him, taking a moment to steady himself so he'd be ready to find his family.

What had they been through? Had it changed them? Did they blame him? Would the love they'd known be the same as it had been before?

A hand touched his shoulder from behind. "Is there something I can help you with?" a woman inquired.

Turning toward the voice, Sergei saw the same soft blond hair and gentle hazel eyes he'd dreamed of for so many nights. The woman was dressed as a servant in a coarse brown dress and white apron, but no amount of plainness could diminish her radiance in his eyes.

"Elana," he blurted, his voice raspy with emotion.

Elana Kremnikov went ashen. "You are a ghost?"

Clutching her hand, he held it to his cheek. "No Elana, it's me and I'm alive, I promise you."

Elana threw herself onto Sergei, pressing her ear to his chest, listening to his thundering heartbeat. Then she drew back, alarmed. "I'm dreaming this!" she surmised.

"No, it's not a dream," he assured her with a light laugh, sympathetic to her disbelief.

Elana threw her arms around Sergei, holding him tightly. Tears rolled down her cheeks but her face shone with joy. "If you are a dream, I don't ever want to wake."

"I tell you, we are not dreaming," he said, stroking her hair.

"If that's so, how can it be? How did you come to be here?"

"An angel sent me to you. How did you get to Paris?"

When she did not answer, he looked down at her and saw she had fainted in his arms.

Once Elana had revived and had come to believe that she and Sergei indeed were reunited, she brought him to the modest chamber she occupied as the monastery's housekeeper. There, in a narrow bed, he saw Peter for the first time in over a year.

"He's gotten big," Sergei noted, holding a lantern

over the sleeping boy. He sat on the bed and swept his hand across the boy's forehead as tears bloomed in his eyes. "I've missed so much time with him," he said in a choked voice.

Elana rubbed Sergei's shoulders to comfort him. "He looks more like you every day," she said fondly.

"Shall I wake him?" Sergei asked.

"Let him sleep," Elana said. "There will be time enough."

Elana sat on a straight-backed chair between her bed and Peter's slim cot and prepared to tell Sergei everything that had happened since they'd left Russia. Sergei seated himself on her bed to listen.

Their carriage had been overturned in a peasants' protest on their way to Denmark. They'd been left on the side of the road as the protesters dragged off the disabled carriage. Elana had tried to continue on by foot, but Peter had become gravely ill with dysentery. If a caravan of gypsies hadn't helped them, he might have died. While Peter recovered, they'd traveled with the gypsies. Along the way, Elana had met a man they knew, and he'd told her that the Red Army had commandeered their estate for a headquarters. "The man told me no one saw you after the Red Army marched into our home. He said everyone believed the Bolsheviks had killed you."

"They turned me out with only the clothes on my back and the few rubles I could hide in my pockets," he told her, "but thankfully they allowed me to live."

"I asked everyone, every Russian person I met,

184

about you," Elana recalled vehemently. "No one had seen you."

Sergei shook his head at the irony of it all. By going off to search for his missing wife and son, he had created a situation that made it impossible for *them* to find *him*. "How did you wind up here in Paris?" he asked.

"The gypsies were traveling through France to Spain. I'm grateful for them. They took good care of Peter; we never would have made it out of Russia on our own. When Peter was well enough, we left them and headed for Paris."

"There are other Russians here in Paris. Did you go to them for help?"

Elana shook her head. "As we were walking into Paris, I developed a fever and collapsed on the road. Who knows what would have happened if some traveling monks hadn't seen Peter crying there by my side. They brought us here and, when I was better, they gave me employment. If I'd had a friend in Paris it would have been different, but I saw no reason to bother people I only vaguely knew when we were really all right where we were."

Sergei glanced around at the Spartan quarters, so different from the life she'd known before. "How brave you've been, Elana," he said, filled with guilt that he had not been able to do more for them. If he had been smarter, more well-connected, more relentless in his search, he felt he could have spared them all this.

Suzanne Weyn

Elana leaned forward in her chair and touched
Sergei's arm. "You know, Sergei, my grief at losing
you was deep. But I have found an inner peace and
quiet happiness here in this monastery that before,
I never would have believed existed. I missed *you*,
but not our old life of superficial acquaintances and
lavish excess."

"That's funny," Sergei said, smiling.

Elana frowned. "I'm not trying to be funny."

"No, I'm not mocking you. Never. I mean . . . I
don't miss it either. I've rather enjoyed living by my
wits without all the pompous grandiosity. But tell
me—don't you find this just a little dull?"

Elana laughed, and to hear that beloved, familiar, wonderful laugh again after so long was almost
too wonderful to bear. "Maybe life with gypsies was
more fun," she admitted. "But I would never want to
go back to the life of the aristocracy."

Sergei chuckled at that. "And a good thing too,
if we ever want to return to Russia. The aristocracy
isn't well liked over there right now. They're putting
everyone who's survived to work."

When he spoke the word "survived" the merriment left Elana's face. She lunged from her chair and
into his arms. Crying fresh tears, she put her arms
around his neck. "I am so happy that you are alive,
my darling. So happy. So happy."

He held her, kissing her soft hair, silently swearing to never let her leave his protection again.

Someone knocked at the door and Elana moved

from his arms to answer it. She spoke quietly to the monk outside her door, and then she turned to Sergei. "Someone has come looking for you."

Elana opened the door wide to reveal a police officer standing behind the monk.

CHAPTER TWENTY-SIX
Blood Memory

Nadya followed the uniformed police officer into a back room of the station house. Ivan lay on a table, a sheet over his body but not over his face. *"Est-il vivant?"* she asked.

"Il est vivant mais passé de hors," the officer replied.

Thank goodness, she thought, resting her hand on her anxiously pounding heart. He wasn't dead but unconscious, probably passed out from the loss of blood.

Then Nadya realized what had just happened. How had she spoken and understood French? She hadn't comprehended what the hotel clerk had been saying to her until she saw the flyer. But the shock of seeing Ivan lying there had jogged something inside her, some buried ability to speak another language.

The police officer told her—in French—that a patrol car had found him bleeding and unconscious on the walkway at the bank of the river. They'd found identification in his wallet and had seen immediately that he was Russian. They'd had an artist execute a quick sketch, which they'd sent to all the hotels, searching for anyone who might know him. Fortunately, Nadya arrived quickly and, as she'd directed them, they'd sent out an officer to find her friend at the monastery.

Nadya understood nearly every word the police officer said, and what she couldn't exactly understand, she could piece together from the context. "Will he live?" she asked the officer, speaking in French.

The policeman told her frankly that, in his experience, wounds like Ivan's usually were fatal.

His words made Nadya reel, and she quickly crossed to the table on which Ivan had been laid, gripping its corner for support. "Have you called a doctor?" she asked.

"Yes, yes, he is on his way," the officer replied as he left the room.

Ivan's white shirt had turned almost entirely red with his blood. Gingerly lifting the fabric, she saw that someone had placed a gauze bandage over the wound, but it, too, was soaked through. On a chair across the room was a pile of white towels. She decided that one of them would be better than the soggy, blood-soaked bandage, as she pulled off her long gloves.

With a replacement towel ready, she peeled away the bandage. To her horror, a crimson torrent began to gush from Ivan's flesh. Instinctively, Nadya jammed the heel of her hand over the gaping injury to slow the outpouring of blood.

Working quickly, she used her left hand to grab the clean towel and press it down on Ivan's chest. A rose-like splotch appeared at the towel's center, but it didn't spread too far. After several minutes, she grew confident that the bleeding had subsided enough to take her hand away. As she withdrew it, Nadya was mesmerized by the red trails of drying blood running from among her fingers, pooling at her palm, and forming streams to her elbow. Her cuticles were rimmed in red where Ivan's blood had seeped under and around her nails.

Just as shock had jolted loose her buried knowledge of French, this sight unlocked another long-bolted door in her mind. Like dreaming while strangely hyperalert, Nadya saw the scene unfold inside her head so vividly it was as though she were living it all over again.

Her eyes crack open and she slowly becomes aware that she is lying facedown on the ground in the woods. The dirt's coolness is like a salve on something burning at the side of her waist. That same flaming agony is blazing across her forehead.

> *She hears a bird's high call.*
> *Above her, leaves rustle.*
> *There's water running somewhere in the distance.*
> *Metal clangs against rock.*
> *With a searing pain in her neck, she forces her head*

around toward the clang. Three Red Army soldiers are waist-deep in a very large hole, digging. Beside the hole is a pile of bodies. Blessedly, their faces are all turned away from her, but she has come awake enough to understand who they are.

She remembers everything now, but knows this is not the time to allow the shattering reality in. To do so would dissolve her into unspeakable grief. This is a moment to think only of survival. For she knows she is one of the corpses the soldiers intend to bury.

Unexpectedly and with animal-like awareness, she is startled to feel a gaze on her. She turns in its direction. A handsome soldier carrying a rifle is staring down at her in alarm. Closing her eyes, she awaits the inevitable shot that will finish her.

A moment passes.

Then another.

There is no shot, so she opens her eyes. The soldier is gone. A little ways off, she hears him being violently sick.

She is nauseated too, but there's no time to focus on it. No one is watching her. This is her chance to move, if she can.

Digging her nails in the dirt, she pulls herself along.

The handsome soldier is returning; she hears his footsteps coming closer. Turning back, their eyes meet. His face is full of sympathy. Somehow she can feel that he is a friend. He turns away again, silently indicating that he won't stop her from leaving.

She's now at the edge of the clearing. The soldiers remain intent on their digging. Their lookout is not alerting them. She is getting away!

Does she dare stand and run? Can she?

She tries. First she's on one knee, and then the other. Pushing forward like a sapling toward a shard of sunlight, she stretches until she is on her feet.

"Hey!"

A shot rings out. It hits her chest so hard her arm flies up involuntarily and her feet leave the ground.

She's thrown backward, and then she's tumbling down the hill that had been behind her. She hits the ground and bounces and is thrown farther down, tossed like a child's rubber ball.

There is more shooting, but she can't tell if it's directed at her. All she knows is that she is moving through space and is helpless to control her direction.

A final bounce hurls her into the rushing river. Facedown, all she can hear is water surging in her ears. The racing tide turns her, face upward, to the sky. She is aware of men shouting, but then the water flips her over once again, and she sees only the silver swirl and froth of the river.

She is carried like this, tossed back and forth, over and over for a thousand years, or at least that's how it seems. Finally the river expels her, shivering and dazed with pain, and washes her onto a dirty, garbage-strewn patch of dirt on the banks of a grimy city.

Coughing river water from her lungs, she climbs to her knees, and then collapses. She dreams deeply of lavish balls and melodic waltzes before falling down a long tunnel of self-protective forgetting.

ᘓ ᘓ ᘓ

It was a horrible memory, but Nadya's unconscious had mercifully held it back until she was strong enough to bear it. Now, looking down at Ivan's pale, still face, she recognized him as the soldier who had been so merciful there in the woods.

Back then she'd owed him her life. He'd helped her to survive, and now he'd plucked her up and brought her home to her grandmother.

It didn't matter to Nadya that she had been a grand duchess. What was a grand duchess—or a duke, or a baroness, or even a czar? They were merely titles. What mattered was that she was a young woman who'd had a family she loved and a life filled with happy memories that were hers to cherish once again.

Overwhelmed with emotion, Nadya threw herself on Ivan's chest. "Don't die," she pleaded. "You mustn't, you can't, not when I finally see you clearly. I love you, Ivan. Stay with me."

She was sobbing so hard into his chest that she was unaware of his right hand gently stroking her hair.

Chapter Twenty-seven
Awake

Ivan opened his eyes and saw that he was lying in a four-poster bed with a lavender satin cover over him. It was certainly far too elegant to be a hospital, yet his torso was circled in bandages.

"Good morning, my friend!" Sergei was seated on an upholstered chair to the left of the bed. "Let me go tell everyone that you are finally awake."

"No, wait! First tell *me* what's happened," Ivan requested.

Sergei recounted how, two days earlier, Ivan had been taken by ambulance to a hospital where he'd undergone many hours of surgery to extract the bullet from his chest. As a result of Nadya's fervent request, the empress had supplied him with the finest doctors in Paris and had allowed him to be brought to her estate to recover.

"Then she's accepted Nadya as Anastasia?" Ivan inquired.

"She has," Sergei confirmed. "They fished that Lepski character that shot you from the river," Sergei went on. "Nadya was still at the police station when they hauled him in, and she identified him. They're holding him on pickpocketing and various other charges until you're able to confirm that he's the one who shot you."

"Where is Nadya now?" Ivan asked.

"Getting beautiful for a ball the empress is throwing in her honor."

"She's already beautiful," Ivan remarked, propping himself onto his elbows. "Come on, now help me up. We're getting out of here."

"No, you can't," Sergei protested. "You're not nearly well enough."

Someone knocked on the door, and Sergei bid them to enter. The maid jumped back slightly when she saw Ivan sitting up and awake.

"Yes, isn't it good news!" Sergei said.

"Very good news," the maid agreed.

"Will you tell the empress that we will be leaving immediately?" Ivan requested.

"Yes sir," the maid said as she left.

"Do you want to reopen your stitches?" Sergei scolded.

"They'll hold until we're back at our hotel room," Ivan argued.

"There's no room for you there."

Ivan looked at his friend incredulously. "What?"

"Elana and Peter are there."

"Are you joking? Of course not! You would never

make a joke like that. Oh, Sergei! My friend! I'm so happy for you. How did it happen?"

Ivan settled back on his pillows to listen as Sergei told him of how Nadya had discovered their whereabouts. Ivan was smiling along with Sergei when another knock came at the door. "Come in," he called.

Empress Marie entered with Nadya behind her. "Then it's true, you're awake! Thank God!" Nadya cried. Although her hair and makeup were done for the ball, she wore a simple blue shirtwaist dress.

"I am awake," Ivan agreed, smiling at her, infused with happiness at the sight of her. How could he go on living without her? He couldn't! He knew it now as never before.

Nadya went to Ivan's side and took his hand. "I was so scared that you wouldn't wake up," she said.

"My maid says that you wish to leave?" asked the empress.

"No!" Nadya cried.

"I don't want to be a burden any longer, though I thank Your Highness for your incredible kindness in caring for me here."

"You are most welcome," Empress Marie replied. "You have brought me my granddaughter, a jewel beyond measure. Your care here is but a small token of gratitude."

The old woman's eyes glistened lovingly as she looked at Nadya. It was easy to see that she'd accepted Nadya as her granddaughter.

The butler entered, holding a polished wooden case that he placed on the dresser and unlocked with a small key. When he opened the case, it was impossible not to be dazzled by the spectacular diamond necklace inside. "Gentlemen, here is your reward for returning my Anastasia to me," the empress announced.

Ivan looked at Sergei, who seemed to have been rendered speechless by the enormity of their prize. It had to be worth much more than had been offered initially.

"This must be the necklace that maniac thought I was carrying," Ivan realized.

"This necklace once belonged to Marie Antoinette," Empress Marie told them. "At one point it was broken, but it has been repaired. I smuggled it out of Russia, along with other treasures, when I escaped from Siberia."

Nadya got off the bed and went to look at the necklace. "I know this necklace! I've been dreaming about it."

"This exact necklace?" the empress questioned.

"Yes," Nadya said. "I remember exactly the large blue diamond at the center."

"Well, it is the most valuable thing I own, so I believe it is fit payment for the return of my most valuable granddaughter. It is all yours with my thanks, gentlemen."

This was his moment for truth, and Ivan suddenly knew just what he needed to do. Spectacular as this necklace was, he could live without it. But he would be miserable if he let Nadya slip away from him.

"We can't take it," Ivan said. "We haven't earned it, because Nadya is not Anastasia!"

"How can you be certain?" the empress asked.

Ivan was surprised by her calmness. Why wasn't the empress more upset by this news? Maybe it was shock or disbelief.

Ivan turned to Nadya and took a breath to steady himself. He had to be completely honest. "Nadya, I was a soldier in the woods on the morning that Anastasia was shot."

"I know. I remember you now that my memory is back," she revealed.

"Your memory is—" Ivan looked at her, perplexed. What was she doing? What new game was this? Had she deluded herself into thinking she really was the grand duchess?

"No, Nadya, you can't remember that because you're not Anastasia," he insisted. "Anastasia was hit in the chest with a bullet, and you have no scar where she was hit."

Nadya gently moved aside the opening of her shirtwaist dress and touched the skin over her heart. "You're right, no scar."

"So you see? You can't be Anastasia." Ivan grabbed both her hands. "I'm sorry for everything that's happened. It was wrong to get your hopes up and to deceive you. The empress could have offered you a wonderful life, but if you don't hate me now, I'll do everything I can to give you a happy life."

"I don't hate you," she said passionately. "I love you."

"I love you, too. I can't be without you. I can never give you what the empress could have, but I swear you won't be sorry I revealed what I know to be true. I'll make up for it in love."

Nadya pulled Ivan to her and they kissed. Even though there were others in the room, while they kissed they existed in a world only they inhabited.

After another moment, the empress coughed, intending to break their embrace. "My dear girl, this might be a good time to show Mr. Navgorny what we found."

"The police gave me your jacket, and I found this in the pocket," Nadya recalled as she took her rag doll out of a pocket of her dress.

"It's your doll!" Ivan said. "Sergei picked it up mistakenly. I meant to return it to you, but obviously I forgot."

"Back in 1917, in the early hours of the morning when we were dressing to go to the basement, I was clowning with my sisters about how much better they looked in their petticoats than I did," Nadya recounted.

"I'm sure you looked just as lovely," Ivan said loyally.

"No, they were older and better endowed," she went on, blushing slightly, "so I equaled the score by stuffing a roll of socks and this rag doll into the bosom of my petticoat. The socks and doll were still there when my father demanded that we hurry. Everything happened so fast afterwards that I forgot all about it.

"The doll's head protected me from the bullet," Nadya continued. "It was sitting directly over my heart when I was shot."

Ivan examined the doll. No, this story couldn't be true. "The doll's head should be shattered, then," he said. "And besides, how can a rag doll protect from a bullet?"

Nadya looked to Empress Marie. "He's right. A plain doll couldn't have."

The empress reached out. "Hand me the doll."

She sees I'm right, Ivan thought. *It's a nice story, but that doll's head wouldn't have survived or protected her in any way.*

Sergei took the doll from Ivan and handed it to Empress Marie. The empress wiggled her finger up under the seam where the doll's head had been sewn on, and she ripped upward. "I recognized this doll as soon as I saw it, because I was the one who gave it to my Anastasia. I knew immediately that it had been altered," the empress explained as she worked. "Now that Ivan has told his story, I understand why."

Empress Marie pulled a hoodlike cover off the doll's head. Beneath it was a bullet-blasted cloth circle—the doll's original head.

Nadya went to Empress Marie's side and touched the doll. "The nurse at the asylum must have repaired it," she realized. "But now I remember the night you gave it to me. You told me to always remember how much you loved me whenever I played with it."

Empress Marie patted her hand fondly. "That's right."

"Wait a minute," Ivan insisted. "How could that soft doll have protected her from a bullet?"

Empress Marie worked her fingers into the center of the doll's head and pulled out a rectangular yellow diamond.

"*This* is what saved her life."

CHAPTER TWENTY-EIGHT
The Diamond Secret

The doctor arrived to examine Ivan, so they had to leave the bedroom. Nadya accompanied Empress Marie back down to the library. The butler followed them in with the necklace, and then left after setting it down on a table.

Nadya absently turned the yellow diamond in her fingers, and then popped it back inside the rag doll before putting its replacement head back on. "There, just as it was," she said, showing the empress.

Propping the doll on the table beside the box, Nadya sat beside her grandmother on the couch. "This diamond belongs to the Marie Antoinette necklace, doesn't it? It came loose," she said as she recalled the fight over the necklace involving Count Dubinsky, Prince Yuperov, Rasputin, and her mother. "I found it later and gave it to you."

"That's correct."

"But there's no missing diamond in the necklace?" she questioned.

"A much less expensive replacement."

"Why didn't you tell me the diamond was in the doll?" Nadya asked. "If I'd known I wouldn't have played around with it so foolishly."

"And you wouldn't be sitting here beside me right now," the empress reminded her. "You have always been a loving girl. I knew if I told you it was a token of our love for each other, you would always keep it close."

"Your idea worked. Maybe, somehow, I remembered what you'd said, even though I couldn't remember anything else. I never could stand to let that doll go. Why did you do it?"

"For the same reason I had the petticoats made. I saw the political signs and suspected that, at some point, we'd have to flee. I didn't want you girls to be left penniless. I hoped to spare you some of what you've been through," the empress explained. "Maybe I should have told you."

"No. You're right. I'd never have had it stuffed in my petticoat if I'd known," Nadya said. "You saved my life, Grandmother." Her eyes misted up, and she laid her head on the old woman's shoulder, as she now remembered doing as a child. Every memory was back: the happy childhood, the loving parents, the terrifying events that could have ended everything. She steered her mind away from thinking too much about her lost parents and siblings. One by one, a little at a time, she would feel her grief and say her good-byes to each of them. Nadya didn't want to be emotionally swamped by taking it on all at once.

"That young man also saved your life," Empress Marie said. "In the end, he was hoping you would turn out not to be Anastasia so that you could marry him."

Nadya lifted her head and gazed at the empress. "Can't we still have that? Why should it matter?"

"It might not matter to you, but it will matter to him," Empress Marie replied. "You can see that he's proud and independent and much more sensitive than he pretends to be. He would never want to live idly off your wealth."

"Then let him work," Nadya suggested.

The empress shook her head. "He could never earn as much as you will have inherited. He would always feel like a kept man, a parasite."

They heard the front door open and close. "The doctor usually stops in to say good-bye," Empress Marie commented. "He must be in a hurry today."

Nadya put her head back on Empress Marie's shoulder. "What do you think will happen next, Grandmother?" she asked.

"I'm not sure," the empress admitted. "It's possible that some loyalist White Russians will want to put you back on the throne."

"I wouldn't like that," Nadya said with certainty. "I've seen a different side of life. Regular life has become part of me. It's fun."

"You always loved fun. That's why your father called you *shvizbik*."

"*Shvizbik*. It means a clown, a joker. I remember! In my dreams he called me that," Nadya said. She sat forward once more. "Grandmother, did you enjoy being a royal?"

The empress's eyes darted as she thought about the question. "No, I did not. I was born a princess in Denmark, but I had to change my name from Dagmar to Marie Feodorovna and leave my family and learn Russian, all because I had been promised in marriage to a Russian czar I barely knew. Your grandfather Alexander was a surly man, no fun at all. I always secretly believed that you inherited your fun-loving nature from me."

Nadya squeezed her grandmother's hand and the two of them silently sat together, contented to feel their closeness. After a few moments Sergei came in. "I have come to say good-bye," he announced.

"You're going back to your hotel?" Nadya asked.

He nodded. "We depart for Russia tomorrow. Elana and I have decided we want to return and start a new life."

"Won't you take your share of the reward?" the empress entreated him. "If not for yourself, then for your family?"

Sergei bowed deeply to her. "I did no more than my duty."

"You're sure?" Empress Marie pressed.

"Quite sure. Besides, I still have much of the

money Count Dubinsky repaid me. We'll be fine. Nadya, I must tell you something else. Maybe we should talk privately."

Before she could reply, the doctor entered, carrying his doctor bag and wiping his chin with a napkin. "Your maid makes a fine borscht," he told the empress.

Nadya jumped to her feet. "If the two of you are here, who went out?"

"That's what I was going to tell you. Ivan wanted me to say that—"

"Ivan left?" Nadya cried.

"Doctor, how could you let him?" Empress Marie scolded.

"He was astoundingly recovered," the doctor said, defending himself.

Nadya ran to the door of the library, but then she ran back. "Where, Sergei? Where did he go?"

"He called a taxi to take him to the docks," Sergei revealed. "He said something about going to America."

"America? He has no money!" Nadya said.

"I gave him some," Sergei admitted. "It was what he wanted."

Nadya did a jig of agitation. "Grandmother, what do I do?"

Nadya saw her grandmother's face cloud over. "Let him go. He's made his decision."

"No, he hasn't," Nadya cried, a terrible pain forming in her stomach. "He's being noble. He thinks he's

doing the right thing, but it's not the right thing—
not for me!"

"He'll be fine," Empress Marie insisted.

"But I won't be fine," Nadya told her passionately. She hung her head and began to cry. "I'll never
be fine again."

The empress went to her side and gently wiped
away Nadya's tears with her soft, gnarled hand. "Then
I suppose you have to go find him," she murmured
reluctantly.

Nadya clutched her grandmother's hands. "But
I've only just found *you* again."

"I am the past. Ivan is your future," Empress Marie
replied. "Do you know what 'Anastasia' means?"

"No. Tell me," Nadya replied.

"It means 'breaker of chains'." Empress Marie
squeezed her lips together. Her expression told
Nadya how much what she was about to say was
costing her heart. "Go break these chains of royal
duty and misery. Go be happy."

Nadya kept hold of her grandmother's hands.
"Do you understand how much I love him? I wouldn't
leave you if I wasn't sure that he's the one."

The empress rapped her cane on the floor so
hard it made Nadya pull back in surprise. "I'm fine!
Go! Write to me."

Nadya kissed the empress's cheek. "I love you,
Grandmother."

Standing, the empress wrapped Nadya in a tight

hug. Her eyes were wet with tears. "Be happy, Nadya," she said.

"I will, Grandmother. Finding you has made it possible for me to be happy again."

Nadya encircled Sergei in a hug. "Good luck, my dear friend," she said.

He kissed her forehead. "Hurry," he whispered tenderly.

Nadya was almost out the door when the empress called to her from the library. Nadya hurried back to where Empress Marie stood with the rag doll in her hand. "You forgot your doll," she said, tossing it to her.

Nadya snapped it out of the air and blew the empress a last kiss before turning to leave once more.

Shielding her eyes with a flattened hand to her brow, Nadya frantically scanned the dock. Her heart skipped when she spied Ivan unsteadily climbing the gangplank of a freighter. "Ivan," she shouted, but the ocean winds carried off her voice, and she knew he hadn't heard her.

The freighter's horn blasted, signaling that its departure was imminent. "Ivan," she shouted, her curls blowing in her eyes as she raced for the freighter.

Finally, when she was at the bottom of the gangplank, Ivan heard her and turned.

His face exploded with joy.

He started to come back down the ramp, but she hurried up and met him halfway. "I'm sorry for leaving without saying good-bye," he explained. "I was afraid I wouldn't be able to leave you if I didn't just go."

"Don't leave me, then," she said with her hands on his arms.

"I have to. You're the grand duchess Anastasia. There's no place for me in your life."

"Not in Anastasia's life, but in Nadya's life there's all the room in the world. Don't you see? I don't want a life without you."

"Are you absolutely sure?" Ivan asked.

"Completely sure," she insisted.

The freighter sounded its horn once more.

Ivan pulled her into his arms and kissed her hard. Nadya held him tight. "You're giving up so much," he reminded her when they pulled out of the embrace.

Nadya smiled up at him. "I'm getting so much more than I'm losing," she assured him.

The freighter's horn blared a third time. "You're sure?" Ivan checked.

"Positive," Nadya said.

Ivan took Nadya's hand, and they hurried up to the top of the gangplank and onto the deck. As the vessel pulled away from the dock, they watched the land recede into the distance.

"We might never see home again," Ivan remarked, wrapping his arm around her shoulders.

"That's all right," Nadya replied, knowing in her heart that, from this moment on, wherever Ivan was would be home to her.

Author's Historical Note

The Russian Revolution began in March 1917 when factory workers went on strike for higher wages. The unrest continued and grew worse, eventually forcing Russia's leader, Czar Nicholas Romanov II, to give up his throne. A provisional Russian government was formed, headed by Alexander Kerensky. But in November 1918, a group called the Bolsheviks, inspired by the communist writings of Karl Marx, overthrew Kerensky. Their leader was Vladimir Lenin. The Bolsheviks did away with the existing Russian government and killed anyone who opposed them.

Czar Nicholas, his wife and four children, his mother, some servants, and a doctor were sent into exile in Siberia. His mother, the dowager empress Marie Feodorovna Romanov, managed to get out of the country, but the rest were moved to a villa in Yekaterinburg, Russia, on the border of the Ural Mountains. There they were all assassinated on July 17, 1918, just as the White Army—the army loyal to the Russian Imperial Family—came to Yekaterinburg in an attempt to free them. Jewels sewn into the petticoats of the four daughters caused the bullets to ricochet wildly around the basement room before the girls were killed.

A rumor that one of the czar's four daughters, the grand duchess Anastasia, still lived was popular in the years following the royal assassination because only the remains of three daughters could be identified when the bodies buried in the woods were uncovered. Women claiming to be the grand duchess appeared in droves, the most famous one being a woman named Anna Anderson. Many stories about what might have happened to Anastasia emerged. Since then, modern DNA testing and new discoveries have proven that Anastasia did not survive that night.

This retelling mixes true history with imagination to create a possible alternate ending to the Anastasia tale. It is a story that the author would love to believe is true.

About the Author

SUZANNE WEYN has written more than a hundred novels for children and young adults and has had her work featured on the *New York Times* bestseller list. Her other novels for the Once upon a Time series include *The Crimson Thread*, *Water Song*, and *The Night Dance*. Suzanne lives in upstate New York. Visit her online at SuzanneWeynBooks.com.

Don't miss this magical title
in the Once upon a Time series!

The
Crimson Thread

By Suzanne Weyn

Once upon a time, I believe it was 1880 or thereabouts, a young princess set sail from Ireland for a faraway land. Bridget O'Malley never knew she was of royal lineage, due to the reduced circumstances into which she was born.

Foreign conquest had brought endless brutal war to the land, and the devastation of this strife, coupled with the dire poverty it left in its wake, had long ago vanquished the line of magical druidic priestesses and high kings from which Bridget was descended. Though she did not appear the part in her rags and cloddish, peat-covered boots, Bridget O'Malley was, indeed, a princess, and, on her mother's side, a distant but direct descendent of the high king Cormac mac Airt of legend.

For anyone with eyes to see, her lineage should have been clear enough. She carried the brilliant, orange-red crown of vibrant, unruly curls that marked all the royal women of her line. She had the unmistakable crystal blue eyes and the spray of freckles across her high cheekbones.

As Queen Avriel of the Faerie Folk of Eire, I have watched these disowned royals, these noble spirits without crowns, for centuries too numerous to count. A descent in fortune may obscure royal lineage in the eyes of mankind, but not so in the realm of Faerie. Here we know that true royalty remains in the blood regardless of fortune's deviations. And so I watch and record the royal ones, despite the fluctuating cycles of rise and fall that they may experience.

Bridget and Eileen O'Malley were my special concern. After their mother died, Bridget and her wee sister were the last princesses of their line. In my ancient Book of Faerie their histories were recorded with no less attention than when their kinswomen of times past wore the Celtic crowns on their heads.

Bridget and little Eileen's lives were hard from the start, and then the Great Hunger struck. When the potato crop failed, the already-dire starvation, poverty, and crushing serfdom spun wildly out of control. The famine left mothers to die in their thatched cottages, their frozen babes blue in their arms. Between 1846 and 1850 droves of starving, desperate families set sail for distant shores. They went to lands known as Canada, Australia, Great Britain, and a place called America. Hundreds of them left, their meager belongings in tow, not knowing what lay ahead, but praying it would be better than the crushing life they'd had.

When Bridget's mother died, her father, Paddy

O'Malley, decided that the time had come to do as so many of his neighbors and kin had already done. He would take his children to America.

And so—invisible to all—I went too, in my role as faerie historian. A strange fate awaited Princess Bridget. I never would have predicted the turns of events that she encountered, being unfamiliar with the magic of foreign lands as I was at the time. For the mix and tumble of exotic magic she experienced was like nothing I could have imagined; nor could have Bridget.

And thus begins this faerie's tale.

As she made her way down the steamer's gangplank, Bridget O'Malley cradled three-year-old Eileen, her younger sister, in the crook of her bent arm. Eileen snored lightly, her head nestled on Bridget's shoulder, her blond curls like a cloud around her peaceful, round face.

With her other hand, Bridget gripped a battered suitcase. It contained everything she had managed to acquire during her seventeen years in the world: two skirts, one of them patched and short, coming just above the ankle, the other, longer one with two rows of ruffles on the bottom, each row added as she grew; a worn-soft plaid flannel nightgown; a few sets of bloomers and undershirts; two faded blouses; a horsehair brush; a blue satin ribbon; a chipped hand mirror; a green and tan blanket of homespun Irish wool crocheted by her mother shortly before her death a year earlier; and two somewhat dull sewing needles.

Bridget squinted against the fierce sunlight. The strong ocean breezes pried strands of curls loose from her upswept hairdo and flung them into her eyes. Setting down the suitcase, she brushed the corkscrews of hair aside.

"Best not let that case stray from your hands, my girl," her father, Paddy O'Malley, advised brusquely in his thick Irish brogue as he stomped down the ramp, flanked by his three sons, nineteen-year-old Finn, thirteen-year-old Seamus, and eleven-year-old Liam. "We've come to the land of thieves and pickpockets."

"Ha!" Bridget let out an ironic laugh. "And here I was thinking this was the land of opportunity. I believe it was you, your very self, who told me so, was it not? Let me think . . . how many times have I heard it?"

"Only a hundred," Finn put in, a smile in his green eyes as he set down one end of the steamer trunk containing all their household belongings and Seamus put down the other. Heeding his father's warning, Finn kept one worn boot propped on top of the trunk.

"No, surely it was two hundred, at least." Seamus continued the joke. He removed his wire-rimmed glasses and gave them a quick wipe on his shirt.

"A thousand times!" Liam piped up. He had the same red curls as Bridget, but his eyes were a vivid green and they sparkled with mischief now, lit gleefully with the fun of teasing their father. "I'm sure he's said it exactly one thousand times."

"Yes, I believe you're right, Liam," agreed Bridget with a grin. "'Land of opportunity'—I believe I have heard that phrase exactly a thousand times."

"And so it is!" Paddy O'Malley insisted, taking his children's teasing in stride. He gazed around at the other passengers who streamed from the ship. They were disheveled and exhausted from the long, cramped trip, dragging trunks and baskets containing all their earthly belongings. Paddy looked on them with benevolent pride, despite their tattered appearance. In his eyes they were kindred spirits, bold seekers of a better life who were now teetering on the brink of incipient riches.

"It is a great land, indeed, and we will find our fortunes here," he said confidently. "But in the meantime, be wary. Keep your wits about you at all times."

Bridget smiled at him as the six of them moved forward with the crowd entering the building. This was a strange new world, and they'd have to learn its ways as fast as possible.

But what could be more auspicious than to arrive at the very entrance of a castle? The Castle Garden immigrant processing center was, indeed, very like a castle. In fact, it had been a fort against the British back during the American War of 1812. It stood at the southern tip of New York City, with two grand rivers on both sides and the very ocean at its door. The glistening building dazzled Bridget with its expansive entryway, elaborate scrollwork, and surrounding wall. Beside the doorway, an American flag flapped in the wind.

They joined the crowd of people moving inside to the great, round center room with its high domed ceiling. "Saints be praised," Bridget muttered under her breath, awed at the sight of the massive room. Even the village church back in Ballinrobe had nothing as grand as this ceiling supported by impossibly thin columns.

They got in one of the many lines and crept forward until they finally reached a desk where a uniformed official sat at a desk with a big ledger on it. Along with her father and brothers, Bridget signed her name in the book, relieved that they didn't ask her to write anything else. Her name was all she knew how to write.

Crumpling his tweed cap nervously in his large, rough hands, Paddy produced a letter from the traveling country doctor attesting that the family was free of disease. He'd made sure to acquire this letter, having heard far too many stories of others who'd endured the grueling sea passage only to be turned back or, at the very least, stuck in quarantine because their health was suspect.

"Address?" barked the official behind the desk, a scowling, thin-lipped man, without looking up from the papers he was filling out.

Paddy O'Malley took a slip from his jacket

pocket and showed the official the address written on it: 106 Baxter Street. His best friend from home, Mike O'Fallon, had been kind enough to rent an apartment for them using money Paddy had sent him. "Mike O'Fallon assures me that it's a fine place," Paddy told the official, "the best he could get for the dollars I sent him."

"The Five Points, eh?" the man said with a grunt as he glanced up for the first time. "Why am I not surprised?"

"Pardon? The what?" Paddy O'Malley asked.

"The intersection of three blocks creates five corners, so they call the area the Five Points. It's the part of downtown you people all seem to head for," he stated with a derisive nod at the others in line. "You can walk there from here; I guess that's why you all go there."

"Are there many others from Ireland there, then?" Paddy inquired hopefully.

"Years ago you people controlled the whole rat-infested slum," said the man, returning to his paperwork. "There was nobody there but a ton of Irish, along with a few Black Africans. But now they're pouring in from Italy, Germany, and all parts of East Europe. You've even got Chinese and Jewish down there nowadays. But don't fret. You'll still find boatloads of Irish there."

Paddy nodded, though a look of worry crossed his face. Bridget understood it. Italians! Germans! Africans! Jewish! Chinese! She didn't even know what an Eastern European was! None of the O'Malleys had ever seen a person who wasn't Irish, let alone someone all the way from China.

The official glanced up for a second time as he handed Paddy a cardboard billfold of entry papers. "You and your boys might find work at the Paper Box Factory at Mission Place," he advised. "And your girl here should check with the House of Industry on Worth Street. They can direct her to the uptown families looking for servants."

"She'll not be a servant," Paddy disagreed confidently, "not one as skillful as she is with a needle."

"Suit yourself," said the official. "Many women go into the needle trades, but she'll have to post a one-dollar deposit with any employer she wants to work for."

"One dollar!" Bridget gasped. Where would that come from? She wasn't even sure how much money it was, but it sounded like a lot.

"That's how it's done. It's why girls hire out as servants," the man said gruffly.

With a nod, Paddy motioned his family to move away from the desk with him. They followed him a few paces until he stopped and faced them. His ruddy face erupted into a brilliant smile. "We did it! We're in!" he exulted.

"Where to now, Da?" Seamus asked.

"On to 106 Baxter Street," he told them excitedly, his face beaming. "The kind gentleman there says it's but a hop, skip, and jump from here. Let us be off. Our fortunes await us!"